The Mysterious Mr. M.

Tommy Nocerino

Dedication

To Teachers everywhere who inspire, encourage and infuse the deep affection for learning.

Acknowledgment

*Special thanks to my nephew Matthew Joseph Nocerino,
my most ardent critic.*

About the Author

Author Tommy Nocerino, a native New Yorker with expertise in American history and American cinema, is often called on as a guest speaker on various subjects. His pop culture commentary is also in demand on numerous internet radio shows. Tommy resides in Fernandina Beach, Florida, and is a teacher of various subjects. With three well-received novels published, he continues to foster and refine his many interests and continues writing.

Disclaimer

Contents

Dedication i

Acknowledgment ii

About the Author iii

Disclaimer iv

Chapter One 1

Chapter Two 8

Chapter Three 17

Chapter Four 24

Chapter Five 34

Chapter Six 43

Chapter Seven 56

Chapter Eight 68

Chapter Nine 81

Chapter Ten 87

Chapter Eleven 96

Chapter Twelve 108

Chapter Thirteen 117

Chapter Fourteen 127

Chapter Fifteen 135

Chapter Sixteen 141

Chapter One

Rudolph Blankenship had a serious dilemma.

The first-year principal at Atlantic View High School in Dade County, Florida, stood outside the burned rubble of the newly built science building. With less than a week, until the new school year started, he had to quickly come up with a plan to get the celebrated science subjects ready and where to put them. More students were set to attend Atlantic High than in its twenty-two-year history.

As the newly appointed principal slowly walked around the large one-story building with twenty-five classrooms and two state-of-the-art laboratories, a fire marshal approached with a camera and cell phone to survey the damage. The fire trucks left less than an hour ago, and the stench of burnt plastic and metal, as well as paint and wood, was still strong. The fire marshal, a tall and solidly built man, put his hand out, introduced himself, and stared at Blankenship.

"The fire company was excited to be at the opening of this building next week. My son's a junior here, ya know," he said.

Principal Blankenship, feeling numbed at the sight, turned to the fireman and nodded.

"Yes. I know who your son is. He's a good student. I was assistant principal here for the past three years and a science teacher here before that." Blankenship cleared his throat and stared at the smoldering smoke coming from one of the windows. "You're not going in now, are you?" he asked.

"No, it's still too hot. I'll take some pictures of the outside of the building first and let it cool down a bit," the fireman answered.

The early morning sky still had smoke hovering over the large campus. The sight was a maddening mood.

The phone rang in the principal's office just as he sat down. He noticed a cup of coffee sitting on the right side of his desk, took the lid off, and sipped. It was made exactly how he liked it, strong with sweet cream. He put it down and thought that he didn't remember stopping for coffee on his way to the school. He needed a few minutes to regain his senses before going back out to speak to the four television news stations looking over the building.

As he was about to get up and go out after taking a sip of coffee, he noticed a handwritten sticky note on the corner of his desk. He glanced at the note and thought about looking at the surveillance cameras around the grounds and the building for any definite clues but decided to wait. Before leaving his office, he again glanced at the note. It read, *'We'll be working on this as soon as possible. It will be completed and better in a few days; I guarantee it.'*

News trucks were trying to get as close as possible, and reporters walked around the damaged building as Blankenship emerged from his office, ready for questions. With coffee in hand, he notices the odd note stuck to the Atlantic View High School cup. Surrounded quickly by news reporters, Blankenship stopped a few feet outside the administration building and was immediately swarmed by the reporters. Holding his head high and ready for questions, he began by saying how the incident would be thoroughly investigated and didn't have any answers at this time.

Reporters pressed the new principal for more answers, being that there was huge publicity touting the new science building and how it would set the standards for all high school science buildings to come.

Blankenship danced around with his answers, talking about the school and how rebounding from this is vital. He was asked what the next step, the real next step, would be and if there was a timetable for repairs. He paused as his right hand felt the sticky note.

Staring at the reporters, he raised his head and proudly exclaimed, "We'll be working on this as soon as possible. It will be completed and better in a few days, I guarantee it."

****

Back in his office, Principal Blankenship sat behind his desk and couldn't believe what he had just said to the reporters. What was he thinking? What compelled him to make such a statement? How in the world did that note get stuck to his coffee cup?

The backlash would be coming, no doubt, he thought. He expected a call from the superintendent first and who knows who else. Two school custodians knocked on his open office door, and he waved them in. They sat quietly in the two chairs in front of his desk. The principal leaned back in his chair and stared at the two men then looked out of his window as the smoke was still hovering over the school.

"It's past sunrise, sir. We raised the flags. We have our checklists. Do you want us to work on them?" one asked a tall black man who had been at the school from his very first year.

Blankenship didn't answer right away.

"Sir?" the custodian asked.

"Yes. Yes. Go to it, men. I'll be here all day if you need me," he answered.

The two nodded and got up and left.

He stared out of the large window and kept thinking about what he just said to reporters. The phone was about to ring off the hook.

Cars began to come into the school's parking lot as teachers, still out on vacation, came back to view the damage and offer support. The principal sat and gathered his thoughts. He wasn't scared. He took a moment to realize his role as a leader, and he had to show it. Two teachers came in and sat in the chairs in front of his desk. At first, the talk was casual about trips and family. Blankenship was glad to talk about the summer, but his thoughts were engrained in the science building.

The two teachers, not part of the science department, expressed their support and made it clear they would be available if needed. He thanked them as they left and sat back down. Exhausted, he sat back in his large chair, placed his hands behind his head, and closed his eyes.

****

As workers were scheduled to begin the arduous task of cleaning up the next day, Principal Blankenship was meeting with the owner of the construction company and the building designer to go over the rebuild. They were reviewing the original blueprints, but the principal had some new ideas, adding more windows and bigger lab space for more hands-on work. As they discussed his ideas, his administrative assistant, Mrs. Sheldon, interrupted to tell him that the insurance adjuster and fire marshal were there.

Walking the grounds and observing the new landscaping, complete with new palm trees all around the huge campus and a new water feature in the middle of the commons area, the insurance adjuster, a middle-aged man with salt and pepper colored hair and goatee, and the fire marshal were quietly discussing the situation. The inspection of the damages had just been completed, and both men were very puzzled. Principal Blankenship approached the two men.

"Well, Mr. Blankenship, this is a tough one," Bradley, the insurance adjuster, said.

The principal looked at the fire marshal.

"Did you find anything?" he asked.

"Nothing I can find. The first time in sixteen years doing this, I'm baffled," the marshal answered.

Bradley shook his head, "We thought maybe it was faulty wiring, but it turns out it wasn't. We're thinking about calling an inspector from the National Association of State Fire Marshals. They can do a more thorough incident collection."

Blankenship wasn't very keen on that idea. "How long will that take?" he asked.

The fire marshal shrugged his shoulders, "Maybe a few days,

depending on their schedule. Maybe longer."

"A few days," Blankenship sadly said. "I've got two cleaning companies coming here. A few days won't work."

The adjuster was puzzled, "What's the rush?"

The principal didn't answer. He just looked at the charred building, then at the adjuster, then at the building again.

****

Two sheriff deputy squad cars slowly drove around the huge campus, and a cleaning company truck entered and parked in front of the administration building. As the fire marshal and Bradley, the adjuster, walked away, Principal Blankenship pushed the door to the science building open and entered. He gazed at the charred rubble, still warm with some smoke rising from the heat. He went into what used to be a classroom. He took his handkerchief out of his back pocket and covered his nose as the smoke gave off a foul smell.

'What a mess,' he uttered to himself.

As he was leaving the oven-like classroom, he thought he heard a commotion in the distance. He made his way outside and heard sirens blaring in the vicinity of the road leading up to the school. Noticing the flashing lights there, he thought the worst. With the speed of an Olympic sprinter, Blankenship raced the two hundred yards to the entrance road and saw a sickening sight - a thirteen-car pileup!

It was the first day of marching band camp, and oddly enough, most of the cars had gotten to the school at the same time. Students were crying, some crawling away from the wrecks as the principal hurried to assist. Ambulances and emergency vehicles quickly made it to the scene, getting at least eight students to the nearby hospital. Sheriff deputies pulled some students to safety, and medical staff administered first aid on the spot.

The band director, Mr. Como, was lying on the side of the road, being attended to by a nurse and a doctor. Blood was streaming down his forehead, and he also had a broken leg. Blankenship knelt next to Como and assured him that he'd be alright and the students would be taken care of.

Two students who suffered minor cuts told the sheriff that the cars were following the speed limit when, all of a sudden, the rear cars started a chain reaction, smashing all the ones in front. A news truck had just arrived, and the cameras began rolling. Parents started to arrive, adding to the confusion, asking questions, and getting in the way.

Four hours later, after the chaotic scene had calmed down, Principal Blankenship walked back to his office. 'What in the world was happening?' he thought.

Chapter Two

In a busy section of Des Moines, Iowa, people were shopping and going about on this warm day nearing sundown. Children were running in and out of an old-fashioned Five and Dime Store, and food vendors on the street were selling things like hot dogs and tacos, filling the air with delectable aromas. Sidewalk and street traffic got heavier on this bright August day.

An elderly blind man with a cane was standing on a corner waiting to cross and didn't know when the light changed, but standing next to him was a tall, distinguished looking man who gently held his arm and assisted him in crossing.

"No worries, my good man. The street will wait," the man said.

The old man, surprised, smiled, "Thank you very much, sir. I'm grateful."

"Have a wonderful rest of the day, Samuel. I know you see things no one else does," the man said.

Smiling, Samuel nodded as they came across, "Odd you should say that I always felt that."

"Well, there you go. Be well," the man answered.

As Samuel thanked him again, he began to walk, then stopped. He didn't recognize his voice; how did this man know his man was Samuel?

A young mother with an infant stroller and a toddler holding her hand came out of a baby clothing store. She realized that she had left her wallet on the store counter and as she quickly turned to go back in, lost her grip on the stroller, and it raced towards the street. She screamed. As it was about to slide off the curb and into an oncoming pickup truck, a hand reached and pulled the stroller back, missing the truck by inches.

"Oh, thank you, thank you for saving my baby!" she exclaimed, shaking from her nerves. "I don't know how to repay you."

People gathered around to see the excitement. The tall, distinguished-looking man gently pushed the stroller to the young mother and then looked inside, the baby sucking his thumb fast asleep.

"Just be more careful, Siss," he replied, not scolding her but sounding encouraging.

The young mother nodded with a tear running down her left cheek. "I will, I will, I promise."

Wiping the tear from her face with his white handkerchief, the tall man smiled, "Now go about your shopping and love your children."

She wanted to give him his handkerchief back, but he was gone. Only her father called her "Siss;" no one else ever did.

****

A burned-out school building and a horrible thirteen-car accident. The newly appointed principal was back in his office trying to sort things out. Car accidents happen; that's just a fact of the roads, but it was very strange was the last car in the line that started the collision did not have any damage in its rear end. There were four students in that car, and they all said that the driver was going well under the fifteen-mile-an-hour speed limit, and they felt as if the car was shoved from behind, not hit, but shoved.

Luckily, the injured students were said to be recovering nicely, but Mr. Como had a compound fracture of his left leg and a head contusion. A new music teacher and band director would be needed right away, so he began writing up a job description for the post. Blankenship checked the clock on the far wall and saw he had about an hour before the school superintendent, Mrs. Natalie Canfield, and the County Sheriff, Ray Hayes, were coming to examine the outside camera footage taken before the science building caught fire.

The new school year was beginning in five days, and an all faculty and staff meeting was in two days. He had to have answers, but most of all, it was imperative that he project confidence and assurance that this upcoming school year would be better than ever. Blankenship sat in his high-back leather chair, took a deep breath, and closed his eyes for a moment. He spun his chair towards his right to the window, then back, then opened his eyes. He was startled.

"Can I help you?" he asked puzzled.

The tall, lean man standing in front of the principal's large desk nodded and smiled.

"Hello. I'm here for the interview. The interview you approved."

Blankenship sat forward. He did not remember any appointment scheduled. He turned to his computer and pulled up his e-mails. Odd, that he didn't see any e-mails about a substitute teacher position request before, but now he sees one with yesterday's date. Something was strange, he thought.

"Yes, well, we can always use good substitute teachers. What's your background?" Blankenship asked.

The tall, stately, stately-looking man was invited to sit down. He smiled, "I have excellent knowledge of many things. Wonderful and different experiences, too. I've worked with scores of people. I help, I help where it is needed; that's in my profile and make-up. I tend to be at certain places where help is needed most."

Blankenship was still puzzled, "Well, this is a great place to be now to be needed," he muttered under his breath. "Have you ever been a teacher? Ever worked with kids?"

"At times. I'm sure you'll find me a refreshing change from what you're used to," he answered. "One doesn't necessarily need to have teaching experience to be a good teacher."

"Yes, but it sure helps. Where did you attend school?" Blankenship asked.

The man proudly raised his head, "I've been on the campuses of Kent State and Virginia Tech but learned a lot at Princeton and Oxford."

"Those schools? Very impressive," the principal responded.

"I'm sure you'll find me quite adequate, Mr. Blankenship."

The principal was still a bit puzzled and looked at his watch as he was concerned at the time, getting close to his upcoming meeting. He nodded and sighed.

"Alright. I'll submit your application with my recommendation," he said.

The tall man smiled, "Thank you, Mr. Blankenship. I will do an exceptional job, I assure you. And that new science building will be amazing, other schools will be copying it. I'll be at the opening of it in two days."

"Well, we'll see . . . wait a minute, two days? That is way too optimistic," the principal said. He looked over the tall man wearing a sky-blue t-shirt under a black suit. His very deep brown hair was slicked back and a bit long past his jacket collar. He thought about the sticky note attached to his coffee cup.

As the new applicant for substitute teacher left his office, Blankenship called in his administrative assistant, Mrs. Nancy Sheldon. The woman, in her late fifties with glasses and with short light brown hair, came in and sat down. She had been the administrative assistant to the two previous principals and was very efficient. Blankenship was extremely glad she stayed on

"How did that guy get in here, Nancy?" he asked. "I don't remember seeing any e-mail about an appointment either until just now."

The woman adjusted her glasses and seemed to be puzzled also. She thought for a moment and smiled.

"Isn't he unusual? Unusual in a clever way. Don't you think?" she said.

Blankenship nodded, "I guess, but how did he get in here?"

"He just showed up, so I let him in. There was something about him that was, well, I can't explain it. I don't know," she said.

The principal looked at his desk and saw a manila envelope with the words "Mr. M.'s Credentials' written on it. He hadn't seen it before and did not remember having it handed to him.

"Something very strange is going on here. I hope I'm not going crazy," he said.

Just then, he looked up and saw the school superintendent and the sheriff standing at his office door waiting.

****

After the school band played The National Anthem and the school's fight song, Principal Blankenship made a brief speech in front of the new science building just three days after the fire devastated it.

An additional room was added in the reconstruction as a crime lab with state-of-the-art DNA data mining like a mass spectrometer, sequencing equipment, a mass spectrometer, a flow cytometer, imaging systems, microtomes, surgical instruments, histology equipment, electrophysiological equipment such as patch-clamp amplifiers, pipette pullers, and analysis software. The entire room was donated by two anonymous people. No other school in the state has such a room.

As Superintendent Canfield began to make her speech, Blankenship glanced over at the new band director and could not stop thinking about how this entire thing came about. He sat and listened, but his thoughts were elsewhere.

After examining and re-examining the video recordings on the grounds of the entire school, nothing was found. Not an image, not a specter. Nothing. The investigation into the building also yielded nothing. That fire had to start somewhere.

Mrs. Canfield insisted that the building be destroyed and rebuilt for the next school year, but Blankenship was adamant that it should stay as is with an attempt to salvage some classrooms. She thought he was being irrational and told him that she would have an estimated cost from a demolition company in the morning to get the work started.

As he sat in his office by himself, the new principal heard a commotion outside as trucks were coming onto the campus and workers were moving about. He quickly got up and went outside with Mrs. Sheldon, going straight for the burned building.

What they saw was something moving like a well-oiled machine: on one end, debris was being carried out and thrown into huge dumpsters; on another end, workers, tools in hand, went right to work. Three foremen were examining blueprints and discussing the job. Blankenship and Sheldon walked over to the foremen and asked what this was all about.

"I got a call early this morning, same as these other guys," one of the foremen said as he shouted out to workers to get a huge sweeping machine going. "The blueprints were in the cab of my truck. "

Blankenship was very concerned, "Who called you?"

"Wasn't it you?" the foreman asked surprised.

Now totally confused, the principal looked at Mrs. Sheldon as two more construction trucks arrived. He didn't sign any construction contracts and never reviewed any blueprints. Workers moved quickly to get the building ready for the renovation, and amid the chaos, a man approached Blankenship and Sheldon. He wore a red plaid suit, a bright red bow tie, a pink shirt, and red sneakers. Mrs. Sheldon thought he looked like the host of a television show for kids. She smiled at him.

"Can we help you, sir?" she asked.

The man, his big broad smile lit up his face, "I got the text just a few minutes ago. I'm here for the job."

"Job? What job?" Blankenship asked.

The man smiled again, "Music director. I'm a music teacher. My name is Wellington J. Ballard. The J is for Julius, but people just call me Ballard."

Blankenship thought he was in an alternative universe. Construction with no approval, at least he didn't approve it; a music teacher shows up without the job being posted, and an applicant for substitute teacher without an appointment. He truly thought someone was playing tricks on him.

Ballard smiled and asked to see the music rooms and said he could not wait to get started and Mrs. Sheldon seemed giddy at his enthusiasm. One of the foremen came over with another well-dressed man.

"This should all be completed by tomorrow morning and the inspections done in the afternoon. You can use the building late tomorrow afternoon," the well-dressed man, the construction company owner, said to the principal. It appeared as if the workers were moving at a phenomenal speed.

Blankenship felt dizzy with all of this. "How can this be? Two days ago, this building was burnt and condemned. Now it's ready? Not possible."

"Well, it's not only possible but done. You said so yourself that this building will be restored in a few days, remember?" the construction company owner replied.

That sticky note on his coffee cup!

Chapter Three

The first day at school at Atlantic View High School was exciting with a large first-year and senior class and a new science building. Principal Blankenship with Dorothy Mullen and Roger Symanski, Assistant Principals, were at the campus entrance welcoming everyone. The students who were injured in the large car accident two weeks earlier were all well and back at school and even participated in the shortened band camp conducted by the new music director, Mr. Ballard.

Three days before, the new principal had a faculty meeting to discuss the new school year and, its expectations and its new motto: One school, one goal - success!

He addressed the recent incidents and proudly proclaimed that hard work and determination turned things around very positively. Though he still wasn't totally convinced about how the new building and new music director came about, he portrayed confidence and had no doubt about getting the results.

As the students filed in, a commotion erupted in the middle of the commons area near the administration building. Students ran and screamed just as water gushed high into the morning air, showing everyone. The three administrators ran towards the chaos getting students back, walkie-talkies abuzz with shouts for security and maintenance assistance. Students, some soaked with filthy water, cried out for their parents as they ran for cover, and calls for emergency personnel blasted the airways. After a little over an hour, the entire student body was in their classrooms, and parents flooded the administration office and nurse's station.

The commotion was calming down as Blankenship and the assistant principals circulated among the parents and students. It appears no one was hurt, just frightened and wet with dirty water. When the incident was thoroughly under control, the new principal sat alone in his office, collecting his thoughts. The door was closed for some privacy.

Closing his eyes for a few seconds, he opened them to see a fresh cup of coffee on his desk. He picked it up to take a sip and felt a yellow stick note on the side of the cup. He took it off and read it. He stared at the odd scribble. 'Keep going. One School, One Goal - Success!' When he looked up, he was startled; it was the new substitute teacher, Mr. M..

"Yes, can I help you? How did you get in here?" Blankenship asked.

Mr. M., dressed in a sky-blue t-shirt under a black sports jacket and black khakis, smiled and pointed to the door.

"It was slightly open, so I came in. You okay? How can I help?" he asked.

The principal was puzzled, "No . . . I . . . I wasn't aware we needed a sub today."

Just then, Mrs. Sheldon came in. She smiled at Mr. M.. and said a history teacher just called in and said he was sorry and would not be in today. They needed a substitute, and she was surprised that Mr. M..

was already standing there. She left the room saying nothing, and Blankenship stared at his uninvited guest.

"I didn't see that you were approved yet by our school board . . .," he said and was interrupted.

Mr. M.. smiled, "Yes, I was. It's there. Pull up your e-mail."

The principal checked his e-mail and saw a notice from the district office of approved substitute teachers. Only Mr. M..'s name was there. He scratched the side of his head.

"I'm not sure of anything going on here lately, but you might want to keep me around to be safe," Mr. M.. said. "Besides, that sewer break will be fixed this afternoon."

Blankenship was getting annoyed, "To be safe? Look, Mr. M.., I appreciate your enthusiasm and willingness to help, but I need a lot more than you to find the underlying cause of all this bad luck we're having so far. I must be snake bit or something."

"No, not snake bit. There is something odd here," Mr. M. replied.

Blankenship chuckled, "Odd? Odd, you say? I'll have to get a rabbit's foot or something."

"If that'll help, why not? I'll keep my eyes and ears open for you."

"Thank you, Mr. M.. Now I'm busy so you better get to your classroom."

Mr. M.. turned to leave, then turned around, "Oh, and by the way, don't go home via Ocean Street this afternoon; take Mermaid Avenue."

"What? Why?" the principal, still annoyed, asked.

Mr. M.. smiled, "Just a thought." He cleared his throat, "It's faster anyway."

As he watched his uninvited guest leave his office, Blankenship slowly shook his head. That guy is getting to be a nuisance, he thought.

Mr. M.. gathered his identification badge and attendance sheets and went to Building Five for the day. He had about ten minutes before the first bell and found that the students, twenty-two of them, were already in their seats or milling around the room. He came into the room and immediately took off his sports jacket, revealing a solid upper body on his six-foot-three-inch frame. The students were shocked that he was wearing a t-shirt and not a collared shirt.

He stood at the front of the classroom and wrote what he expected to be called Mr. M.. As he watched the class slowly settle down so he could call the roll, he noticed a student still standing and talking and not paying attention to what he was expected to do - sit down.

"Young man, we're waiting for you, be seated, please," Mr. M.. politely asked.

The boy chuckled and made a funny face to the girl behind him. He glanced around the room and scratched his head.

"It's the first day. I think I sit over there," he said, pointing to an empty desk near the window. "Oh wait, I think I sit over there," he said again, pointing to an empty desk near the door.

Mr. M.. nodded, "I think you'll sit at the desk right where you're at.”

“I can’t, ya see, I just can’t get myself in it,” the boy answered, laughing as the rest of the class wasn’t amused now.

Suddenly, the boy wiggled back and forth and was slammed into the desk. Startled, the boy’s eyes popped, his eyebrows raised in surprise.

“How did that happen?” he yelped.

Mr. M.. then completed calling the class roll and began teaching, to the astonishment of the students, as it was the first day and nothing was expected. He talked about the Roman Empire and its contribution to the present day, mesmerizing the students with his precise, accurate descriptions of the Roman Aqueduct and Coliseum and life in the ancient city.

When the bell rang for the end of the period, the students got up to leave, thanking Mr. M.. for his wonderful stories. The problem student was still in his seat.

“I can’t get out. I don’t know what the problem is, but I can’t move,” the boy said.

Mr. M.. shook his head, “Well you better figure it out because another class is coming in, and you don’t want to be late for your next class, do you?”

“I’m stuck,” he answered as he jostled back and forth and tried to get up, lifting the desk slightly off the floor.

The next class filed in, looking over the substitute teacher and laughing at the sight of the boy trying to get out of the seat. The bell rang, and the boy popped up and raced out of the classroom.

"Good morning, I'm Mr. M.., your guest teacher for the period. Let us begin," he said with a smile.

****

A week went by smoothly, but Principal Blankenship always had this feeling that something else was going to happen. The broken sewer line under the commons area was fixed quickly that same day, and the area was restored as good as new. He never was one to look over his shoulder and didn't want to start now. His assistant principals kept assuring him that these mishaps were just flukes and not to worry. He also noticed that the new substitute teacher was on campus early every day and took any class assigned. Was there something unusual about this guy, or was it just his intuition to keep an eye on him? He thought. When he mentioned Mr. M.. to Mrs. Sheldon, she would gush about how cooperative and courteous he was and always available to come.

One day, at the end of the school day, Blankenship saw Mr. M.. leaving a bit later than usual and stopped him.

"Late, aren't you? Is everything okay?" the principal asked.

Mr. M.. smiled, "Maybe so; I was discussing the Code of Hammurabi with Mr. Carlson. Fascinating teacher that Mr. Carlson."

"Yes, I know, very bright teacher. The students like him a lot, too," Blankenship said.

Mr. M.. nodded, "You know he also has a master's degree in forensic science and once worked for the District Attorney's office."

"Yes, I . . . er," he was interrupted.

"It's okay if you didn't know that. Not many do. He would be a great addition to your science department with that new crime lab. Don't you think?"

Blankenship thought for a moment and nodded, "Yes, that would seem to be a good idea. I'll think about it. I would have to get a teacher to cover his history classes, though."

"Don't think too long about it," Mr. M.. answered to the ire of the principal.

"Oh, and by the way, how did that route via Mermaid Avenue go last week?"

Blankenship pursed his lips and looked out the window, "Really good, there was a big accident on Ocean Street, and I actually got home faster on Mermaid. How did you know . . .," he looked up, and Mr. M.. was gone.

Chapter Four

Mr. M. was not odd. He was just a product of his birth and environment. His father, a free-spirited wizard, and his mother, a very practical mortal, had a challenging time understanding what she was actually in. Her husband was a good man, very unconventional, with a penchant for gambling and a protective father-in-law, which made her life unpredictable.

In a time that had no real date to record, they were married on the Celtic Island of Eire, present-day Ireland, on a beautiful spring afternoon with a multitude of guests, each one a bit strange. Her new sister-in-law, with long flowing chestnut brown hair and slim in a light blue gown, looked as if she belonged in an ancient time.

Abelgood, her father-in-law, had a white beard, snow-white hair, and a narrow face. There was something Homeresque about him, and he was respected by everyone. She was told they could live anywhere they pleased further puzzling to her.

They quickly had a son, and since Abelgood did not trust his son to show the boy their ways, he took the boy under his wing and taught him the finer points of using his powers for good against the evils of the world. Since the boy was part mortal, he did not have full powers, and lessons were different. The boy would have certain feelings these Gaelic wizards didn't have, especially feelings of love and sorrow. As the boy grew, he embraced his powers and used them for good, never forgetting his grandfather's tutelage. A scholar in world history, mathematics, languages, and literature, his purpose was evident:

assist, be part of the solutions, and never be the problem.

The Atlantic View, High School Band was preparing for its first concert and was rehearsing outside in the Commons area after school. The large, enthusiastic orchestra was not fazed at all at the unusual heat that afternoon, and the program was to pay tribute to Mr. Como, who was convalescing from his injuries from that big car accident. The orchestra followed the arrangement of the new director, Mr. Ballard, to the very note. The excitement for the concert was mounting.

An uninvited guest had shown up standing by the administration building listening to the melodies and became concerned: he didn't recognize the band director. He immediately went inside to see Principal Blankenship.

Mr. Chester Gald, Assistant Principal at a rival high school and brother-in-law of the school council president, interrupted Blankenship while he was on the phone with the superintendent. Irate, he politely waved Gald to sit. He knew Gald didn't like him for the mere fact that Gald was up for the principal position along with Blankenship. Getting off the phone and quickly getting ambushed for hiring a new band director not yet approved by the school board, Blankenship had enough and asked the irate Gald to leave. He wouldn't. The discussion was getting heated when a visitor showed up.

Both Gald and Blankenship looked up and were puzzled at Mr. M.. standing at the doorway. He was delivering a manila envelope to the principal, and as he handed the parcel to him, Mr. M.. looked Gald up and down. Gald, with a sour look on his face, stared at Mr. M. Blankenship, smiled, and handed a notarized sheet of paper to the annoyed assistant principal. Mumbling some obscenity, Gald huffed and left the office before shouting he'd get to the bottom of this. Mr. M.. smiled at the principal and left his office.

Days went by, and the school year seemed to be going smoothly when the football team ran into trouble. Mr. M.. was subbing an English Honors class when a player on the team mentioned to him that the first game of the season might have to be postponed due to their facilities. It appeared that the two practice fields and the stadium field were covered with six inches of water.

Odd since it hadn't rained in over a week. The sprinkler systems were never turned on, and what made it more puzzling was the fact that the practice fields were not even close to the stadium. The head coach, Roger Carson, and his assistants, angry at the sights, had to scramble to get a practice field, and time was running out.

At the end of the school day, Mr. M.. walked out to the practice fields and saw Blankenship standing there. Shaking his head, Mr. M.. knew exactly what he was thinking. The football players, in their practice uniforms, gathered around the north practice field and were despondent.

Mr. M.. took off his navy blue sports jacket and held it over his shoulder. Some of the players were talking to Blankenship and were unaware of what had just happened. With their backs to the fields, the six inches of water evaporated, and the green grass glistened in the afternoon sun. A student came running from the field house and said the stadium field was suddenly dry!

Blankenship looked around and saw Mr. M.. talking to some of the players. He just couldn't understand any of this. He walked towards the players, and the rest of the team jogged out, surrounding the principal as he walked. Mr. M.. passed Head Coach Carson and casually remarked to watch the "flea-flicker" in the fourth quarter. Carson, surprised, thought the substitute teacher was kidding. Blankenship looked around to seek out Mr. M.. and he was gone.

****

The senior honors American History class was settling down in the first period one sunny morning and were a bit disappointed that their teacher was out and Mr. M. was their sub. Their topic was early twentieth-century economics and the rise of unions. As the students watched a brief documentary, Mr. M.. paused it. He began describing the first Union in Philadelphia formed by shoemakers in 1794 and how industrialization contributed to their growth. He then stared directly at the back wall.

With its posters of the signing of the Declaration of Independence, portraits of George Washington and Abraham Lincoln, and a rare poster of the signing of the surrender of the Japanese in World War Two, he stared as the students immediately fixed their total attention on him. He began to speak.

"On March 25, 1911, The Triangle Shirtwaist factory workers were about to end their day. Five hundred workers, mostly Italian and Jewish immigrants working for between seven and twelve dollars a week, and ages from 14 to 50, began to clean up," he said, his voice changing slightly deeper, his face an unusual glow. He continued.

"The Asch Building on Washington Place in Greenwich Village, New York City, had ten floors, and floors 8, 9, and 10 were occupied by the Triangle Shirtwaist Factory. Hot, crowded conditions made the nine-hour workday unbearable at times, but these women were grateful to have work. As the women were gathering their belongings and cleaning up, a telephone call from an 8th-floor bookkeeper said there was smoke coming from their floor. However, the other floors didn't get a call or even an alarm," he said, still staring at the wall. A student interrupted him.

"What's a shirtwaist?" she asked.

Mr. M.. nodded, "A lady's shirt or blouse with a collar and cuffs. It was the style for a while, and then it started to lose its appeal." He looked around the room and noticed that the young students in the room were about the same age as most of the victims in that fire. He continued with their total attention.

"When the fire started, flames overtook the floors, and the two freight elevators were working at a furious pace to get as many people down as possible. One of the stairway doors was locked to prevent people from taking breaks there, and the supervisor with the key left the building and escaped," he said, taking a breath.

"Women were jumping out of the windows to their deaths to escape the sweltering heat from the flames. The fire department's ladders could only go to the seventh floor, and women crowded on the one available fire escape that couldn't hold the weight and toppled to the ground, killing 20 of them.

A sound more terrifying as a body slamming onto the concrete pavement has yet to be heard said many witnesses. A good Samaritan that stayed behind led two dozen women to the roof where they were able to jump onto the adjacent building, their bodies slightly scorched, but they survived."

He continued to describe the horrifying screams and sights as desperate women jumped from the Eighth and Ninth floors to get away from the suffocating heat. Fire departments on the scene were useless as their ladders only went up to the Seventh floor, which was already engulfed in flames.

Mr. M.. gazed upward for a moment. His silence ended his description of one of the deadliest industrial disasters in New York City history, captivating the entire nation. He then went on about the aftermath of how hundreds of healthcare workers from around the city descended on the site to help the injured.

After a few questions, he went on to say that the Triangle Shirtwaist Fire changed working conditions and more serious safety inspections in factories to this day.

At the end of the school day, Mr. M.. sat in the classroom and wrote brief notes for the teacher in each class. All good, positive notes. As he was writing, three students came into the room.

"Hi, Mr. M.. Can we come in?" Rosalind called "Rozzie," a senior in one of the day's classes asked.

Mr. M.. smiled, "Oh, sure. C'mon in."

The three students, all seniors and honor students, were in his classes that day. They sat at the desks directly in front of the teacher's desk.

"Mr. M.., you described that fire, that horrible fire, as if, well, it was almost like you were there," Rosemary, one the students sitting, said.

Mr. M.. looked at her and the other two, "It was a horrific event. One that should never be forgotten. The city dedicated a museum to the incident."

"Mr. M.., while you were talking, I could almost see the entire fire in front of me. I never felt that way," Ryan, a tall, lanky student wearing an Atlantic View Football t-shirt, said. "You must really research things."

Rozzie shook her head, "It must have been . . . ." She was interrupted.

"Yes, it was. It was one of the deadliest, and, well, things like that happen to change things. Unfortunately," Mr. M.. said.

Mr. M.. smiled and sat back, "Hey, tell me, who's that student with the thick glasses and plastered-down hair? I think his name is Harvey Humble?" he asked.

"He's a new student, transfer, I guess. He is in my chemistry class and my elective forensic science class," Rosemary said.

"He keeps to himself. I think he's very smart, though."

The teacher was curious about him because of the odd questions the student was asking about the Triangle Fire. Questions about describing the faces of the victims and to describe how the bodies slowly burned. The student wanted to hear graphic descriptions, and Mr. M.. would not have any of them.

Ryan got up to excuse himself to go to football practice, and he said he would meet up with the two girls later to do homework. Rozzie watched him leave the room, and Rosemary commented about Ryan not asking Rozzie out on a date, embarrassing her. The two girls then began talking about their friend, Ryan Alworth.

Rosemary looked at Mr. M.. as he was finishing his writing.

"That's a good guy, Mr. M.. He studies hard and plays sports for school. He is fairly good, too," she said. "He has it tough, though. He lost his parents to a car accident when he was three years old, and it's been his grandmother bringing him up. She's been sick now; it's her heart."

Mr. M..'s ears perked up, "Just his grandmother, you say?"

"Yes, just his grandmother," Rozzie answered."

Mr. M.. looked at his watch and noticed it was time for him to sign out, so the students would have to go, but he told them that they were always welcome in any classroom he was in.

As he walked outside to the administration building, he passed football coach Carson. They exchanged pleasantries, and as the coach walked past, he stopped.

"They tried the flea-flicker in the fourth quarter. We were ready for it and stopped them, an interception. Our first win," Carson said with a smile. "How'd you know that?"

Mr. M.. just smiled and nodded.

Just then, the fire alarms went off all over the entire campus, forcing clubs and the band to go outside, causing havoc. Mr. M.. turned around and headed towards Building Three.

****

The meeting at the county board of education building was odd. Mr. Gald was discussing the school term when he brought up Atlantic View High School with Superintendent Canfield and his brother-in-law, Jerry Barron, the president of the school board. Gald was spouting about how Principal Blankenship is incompetent and is the reason these occurrences are happening at that school. He said he's been personally keeping his eyes on that school and knows how to fix its problems. He strongly urged a school board vote to replace Blankenship.

As days went by into the school year, Mr. M.. was at Atlantic View High School every day. He subbed for various classes and kept them captivated with his descriptions of events related to the subjects at hand. As he was writing brief reviews for the teacher, he filled in for the three students, Rosemary, Rozzie, and Ryan, who came in to just say hello.

Mr. M. asked how things were going, and the two girls, both exceptional students, started talking about their Honors English teacher, Mrs. Hamilton.

"She wrote me up two weeks ago just asking to borrow a pen. My pen ran out of ink, and she wrote me up. Then two days ago, she apologized and said she formally retracted it," Rozzie said.

Rosemary added, "She's been bringing in treats every day, too.

She's even dressing differently, more modern."

"I wonder what's gotten into her?" Rozzie said, looking at Mr. M..

Shrugging his shoulders, Mr. M.. slowly shook his head.

Then it happened – the alarms around the school went off!

Chapter Five

Principal Carl Blankenship sat alone in his office and stared out of the window. Never a superstitious man, he couldn't help but think he was truly jinxed. The newspapers and television crews had just left, and the meeting with Superintendent Canfield and his two assistant principals to discuss the next step in cleaning up the latest disaster didn't go well, it seemed.

The entire ceiling of the cafeteria collapsed, and though there were no injuries, the superintendent voiced her frustrations at the horrible occurrences. She could never blame Blankenship but, in a way, expressed doubts about the leadership. She hinted that maybe a change would be due to offset the negative "mojo" in the air.

The plan was to clean up the building as soon as possible and get tents and food trucks for the students, all at a huge additional cost. The roof would have to be repaired, and the insurance adjuster was on his way once again.

The principal turned away from the window and saw his coffee cup filled. He thought it odd that it was as he never filled it. He took a sip. It was just the way he liked it. He looked up to see Mr. M.. standing there. Annoyed, he pursed his lips and began to express his irritation at Mr. M.., just barging in without asking. Blankenship looked at the reminder note about the emergency school board meeting coming up the next evening and shook his head. Calmly, Mr. M.. spoke, and though still annoyed, Blankenship listened.

****

American History Honors class had a spirited discussion about the battle of Gettysburg as the students went back and forth about the final day, Pickett's Charge, and whether it played a necessary role in the outcome to save the Union. Mr. M.. was subbing for Mr. Halliday and posed questions after his precise description of the three days of battles in that small Pennsylvania town.

One student, Harvey Humble, making his usual outrageous statement or asking an odd question, kept raising his hand and adding that the South could have won the battle if they had used certain tactics, things Mr. M.. was unaware of. He also said that the North should have let the South go and maintained their way of life, seeing nothing wrong with it. This caused a huge outcry among the entire class.

Humble, he very calmly took criticism and harsh words in stride, never wavering from his statement. Mr. M.. was very curious about this student and thought Humble was just a person who wanted to get people going and get under their skin. Humble seemed highly intelligent, more so than other students. He also felt that Harvey Humble was a kind of adversary anytime he had him as a student.

At the end of the day, Rozzie, Ryan, and Rosemary came by his class just to talk. They would ask him personal questions, which he evasively answered. He also mentioned how great the cafeteria looked after it was cleaned and refurbished overnight. They agreed it was a miracle. Ryan had to leave for football practice and mentioned that boys' basketball tryouts were going on in the gym. Mr. M.. became concerned, finished his reviews, and went to the gym.

The school's gymnasium, a huge, detached building with new scoreboards and plenty of seating, had two hours of tryouts for the boys' team. As Mr. M.. walked by outside the gym, he noticed a student, his head down and distraught, leaving. He stopped him.

"How's tryouts, Jimmy?" Mr. M.. asked the student.

The boy, about six feet two inches tall and wiry built, shook his head, "No good for me. I can't dribble very well and my shooting, well, it's weak."

Jimmy Davis was a first-year student and a good student. He was the youngest of three boys, and his older brothers were exceptional athletes. He felt ashamed that he would go home and tell them that he didn't make the team.

"Not good, you say? You tried very hard, didn't you? In fact, you try very hard in everything you do. You give up a lot for someone your age. You volunteer at the food bank, right? You could be doing things with your friends, but you go there," Mr. M.. said.

Jimmy was puzzled, "How'd you know that?"

"You give up time with your friends there," Mr. M.. answered with a smile. "I tell you what, go back to the gym. Go over to Assistant Coach Williams and take the ball he is holding."

Jimmy shook his head, "Tryouts are almost over; it's too late."

"Nonsense. Go in, take the ball. Dribble, cross over, dribble, and take a long shot. After you get the ball going through the hoop, stuff it, jam it, slam, and dunk it. Jam it with your right hand," Mr. M.. said, nodding. "From now on, you'll be that player, exactly that player."

Feeling empowered by this substitute teacher that he had never met, Jimmy Davis went into the gym. As the tryouts were about done, he took the ball out of Assistant Coach Williams' hand and did exactly what he was told. To his surprise, the entire gym, with coaches and students, yelled and applauded. Assistant Coach Williams went over and told Jimmy Davis to be at practice tomorrow at four o'clock and ready to play on the varsity.

Mr. M.. stood and watched, but he was really concerned about the gymnasium. With all that was happening around the school, he felt he had to be in the right place at the right time from now on.

****

Chester Gald and his brother-in-law sat in a diner on Sea Breeze Avenue, having a late afternoon dessert of pie and coffee. They were discussing the upcoming board meeting, and the plan to have Principal Blankenship replaced with Gald. His brother-in-law was uneasy about the whole thing, knowing that the recent disasters were not Blankenship's fault, but he did not want to upset his close family member. Gald, short of stature, slightly bald with salt and pepper hair and glasses, was confident he would get the entire board on his side. He waited for the meeting with great anticipation.

Mrs. Sheldon had just finished typing Principal Blankenship's address to the board and was about to print it out for him. She looked over the three pages and noticed Mr. M.. standing next to her, startling her. She looked at him endearingly and smiled as he convinced her to go home after putting in a long day. She printed the three pages and left them after placing them on Blankenship's desk. Mr. M.. looked over the words and placed his right hand on the side of his face, tapping his forehead with his index and middle fingers. He shook his head and slowly waved his left index finger back and forth. As he was about to turn away, he stopped and waved it again, then smiled.

The meeting room was packed with people: parents, a local newspaper reporter, the sheriff, and the county supervisor. People settled in, and the meeting began with the pledge of allegiance and an invocation from a local minister. Principal Blankenship sat in the front row next to Mrs. Sheldon and three teachers, and Mr. Gald sat in the front row on the other side of the aisle.

Superintendent Canfield opened the meeting with a long statement about the state of the schools, the dedication of the teachers, and how attendance is up in the first two and half months of the school year. She ended with her concern about Atlantic View High School, mostly about the safety of the students. She explained that these accidents were oddities that still could not be explained and assured parents that they were taking every safety precaution. The Board President then thanked her for her opening and asked if there were any issues to be discussed, which was a cue for Mr. Gald to stand up and be recognized.

Babbling on about school safety and the seriousness of the recent incidents, Gald posed the insistence that Principal Blankenship be removed and the board appoints a new principal now. Gald stressed the fact that Blankenship has done nothing to assure families of their safety each day, hindering their learning process. His point was that the students are preoccupied with safety, not their studies. He said that he would be a better choice and guaranteed that these incidents would end with him as principal. The board was leaning towards Gald's points and appeared to agree to remove the new principal when Blankenship was pinched on his bottom and jumped up. The board president recognized the principal. Slowly turning his head to look over the room, Blankenship began to speak.

Mrs. Sheldon walked directly into the principal's office the next morning instead of going into her own. She saw Blankenship looking intensely over his e-mails, so she cleared her throat to get his attention.

"You know, last night during the meeting, we had an incident here," he said. "There was a fire reported in the field house."

Mrs. Sheldon was aghast, "There was what? A fire?" she asked.

"Yes. I had my phone turned off, so I did not get the alarm or the call. It was put out or something. Anyway, there was no damage, according to the chief," he answered.

Mrs. Sheldon shook her head, "It's sabotage, you know. Why are we being a target?"

"I don't know, but I'm going to try hard to get to the bottom of all this," he said.

Mrs. Sheldon then changed her tone to one of elation, "I didn't get a chance to tell you how wonderful you spoke last night. They were out to get you."

"Thank you. Odd though, I don't remember writing that address," he said.

The secretary smiled, "It was wonderful."

Mrs. Sheldon then left the office, and Blankenship turned his chair and looked out the window. He took a moment to think about the night before. There was a feeling, a feeling he had never experienced as he spoke to the board and the entire room, for that matter. When he inexplicitly jumped up, he was embarrassed at first, then became overcome with confidence. He took over the room and began:

"I've been hearing about these occurrences as if they're the fault or negligence of a person. That someone isn't doing or can't do their job. Well, that person is me. Atlantic View High School has had a run of bad luck in some things, but everyone in this room fails to see or, better yet, even acknowledge what the school has done so far," he proudly said, sensing he had the undivided attention of the entire room.

"Students are preoccupied with safety, which is hindering their learning process, you say. Tell me where this school had more team participation and more club participation; yes, we've added four more clubs for students to join, and they are joining. Attendance has been higher than any time in the school's history, and truancy and absences are down," he said.

The room was trance-like at this point.

"Grades are at the top of the state's requirements, a real testament to our teachers and staff. You all are missing the very point of why we're here. Instead of celebrating the success of our school, you want to cow-tow to someone who is clueless as to what we do."

The entire room looked towards Mr. Gald.

"There's been some occurrences. Did any of you ever think that with all that destruction, the clean-up and repairs were done in a record-breaking manner? You make a change now, and you just might strike at the very heart of each student. Their spirit. The spirit of our students should be embraced, nurtured, bad luck be damned. You people will decide now, but just remember; it's about the well-being of the students. It will always be about the students."

There was one clap heard, then another, then another, until the entire room applauded. The board president immediately exclaimed that no vote was needed, and the meeting was adjourned. Then, the board president banged the gavel down.

Blankenship kept staring, and a thought quickly came to mind: that address to the board was not the one he had prepared. His apology and humble appeal to the board were to let him stay as principal. There has got to be a sensible explanation.

Mr. M.. sat at the desk in the den of his house and was reading The Canterbury Tales by Geoffrey Chaucer, a masterpiece satire of life in England in the Fourteenth Century. He took some notes as he read. Laying down alongside him was Camelot, or "Cam," his faithful German Shepard, and sitting at the right corner of the large maple desk was Bogo, a two-foot-tall blue and orange gargoyle. Bogo was a gift from his grandfather. Mr. M.. looked up and noticed Bogo staring at him. He shook his head.

"I can't get anything past you. Why did you have to be so smart?" he asked the diminutive being.

Bogo smiled, made some squeaking sounds, and flapped his blue wings.

"I know, I know. I must be careful. You are right," he said, understanding Bogo's high-pitched sounds.

The gargoyle smiled and squeaked on advising his friend about the present problem.

"You are right again. There is a bigger problem I'm tasked to solve here, so I can't get caught up in any real human stuff. Being half-human is hard," he said.

Bogo flew off the desk and glided around the room, making a humming sound, and then landed back on the desk. He smiled at his friend, pointed at a book on one of the hundreds of books in the bookcases, and floated the book to the desk in front of Mr. M..

"Romeo and Juliet?" Oh no, not that one!" he gruffly replied.

Chapter Six

The in-school detention room had three students for the day. One of the students, Leonard Rowdin, who was also the student who gave Mr. M.. trouble the first day when he wouldn't sit down, was a known classroom disrupter and had overall pain in the neck. He sat quietly stewing, plotting revenge against the substitute teacher that sent him to detention – Mr. M.. It seemed that the day before, Mr. M.. was subbing for algebra class, and Leonard Rowdin, Jimmy Jameson, and Zach Breen were acting up, causing trouble.

The three students always stayed together and were not liked. Mr. M.. politely told them three times to act like young men, and when they ignored him, the oddest thing happened: their mouths were sealed shut as if they were glued. He wrote about the incident in his class review, and the next day, the teacher sent them to the detention room. Now, Rowdin thought about getting back at the sub.

The football team was in the playoffs for the first time in five years, and the school was excited with a huge pep rally planned for the next day. Banners were made and placed all over the halls. As practice was about to begin, a swarm of wasps, thousands of them, attacked the field as a few players took off, running back into the field house to safety.

Coach Carson stared out the window and saw the entire practice field, one hundred yards, completely draped with wasps. He'd have to call off the practice at a most crucial time, but he thought about having it in the gymnasium, so he sent an assistant to see about it. He returned, saying the gym doors were stuck and that the key wouldn't work.

As Mr. M.. was walking to his car near the gym, he noticed the huge swarm hovering over the field. He shook his head and walked over. Standing about five feet from the humming horde, he pointed his index finger at the swarm and slowly moved it back and forth. In an instant, the humming stopped, and the wasps disappeared. Coach Carson and his assistants came out of the field house bewildered. Mr. M.. went to his car and watched the entire team run out onto the field.

****

At the end of the next school day, when the wasp incident was talked about to exhaustion, Mr. M.. was walking through the hall of Building Four and noticed Mrs. Hamilton sitting at her desk. He passed the room, then stopped and went to the doorway. He cleared his throat, and when she didn't react, he knocked on the open door. She looked up over her glasses and still did not respond. Before knocking again, a magnet fell from the whiteboard, making her look up at him. He slowly walked towards her.

"You don't like me, Mrs. Hamilton. That's been obvious," he said as he stood about three feet from her desk. "That's a shame. I would certainly feel honored if you did like me."

Surprised at that statement, Mrs. Hamilton raised her eyebrows. She was almost sixty-five years old, had dark hair with streaks of gray, and always wore light makeup. Her nails were always perfectly manicured, and it was obvious that she tried hard to keep a youthful appearance.

"Why would I be so important to you?" she asked gruffly. I don't know if you matter."

Mr. M.. smiled, "Well, I guess I don't matter to most people; that's alright with me, but you, well, you're different. It's been a hard road for you."

"What? Hard road? Nonsense," she answered.

Mr. M.. sat on the top of a nearby desk.

"Yes, it's difficult to realize it not just for you but for all of us at some time. You weren't always this kind of person. It only takes one event, one incident, or even maybe one spoken word to change a person's outlook on things. On life." Mr. M. smiled at her. "Gladys Hamilton, that one incident years ago changed you as a person. But it's never too late to adjust and be yourself."

Mrs. Hamilton put down her pen and took her glasses off. She stared at Mr. M.. for a moment and looked into his eyes. They seemed to change color from green to blue to hazel, then to a flame-like blue. She sighed.

"You know that?" she asked as she looked down.

"I was in love with Douglas Benning when we were both in college. We were to be married when we graduated, but he was found dead after contracting spinal meningitis two days before our wedding. I didn't handle it very well. I blamed myself. Silly, isn't it to blame oneself for another's illness?" she said, now looking at him.

Mr. M.. smiled and nodded as she went on. "I never married after that. Oh, I wanted children, a family, but couldn't bring myself to it."

He looked up, then at the teacher and smiled.

"When someone has a tired heart, it is difficult to function. You felt as if your world was over when Douglas Benning died, so you immersed yourself in the field of education to fulfill a way to be needed, only you took a bad path. You treated your students terribly over the years," he said.

Mrs. Hamilton wiped a tear from her right cheek.

"You see that, and I guess you've heard students talk," she said, looking at him. "I can change."

Mr. M.. smiled, "Start now. Forget that surprise quiz. You were going to spring on the classes tomorrow, and how about not having homework on the weekend? Just a suggestion. Take each student for what they are: just teenagers with feelings like everyone else."

"I've never told any of this to anyone, ever," she said, leaning forward. "You seemed to know, though. I feel so much better talking about it. Thank you for stopping to talk, Mr. M.."

Mr. M.. stretched his long arms, "And by the way, that man who lives in the condominium across from you, Mr. Peter Simanski, you know that retired chap who's been very friendly towards you? Well, you'll be very surprised to know that he's a widower and would be pleasant company."

The next day, Mrs. Hamilton was in the teacher's break room talking to three other teachers before classes started. The three teachers were surprised that Mrs. Hamilton stopped them and engaged in pleasant conversation.

The exciting pep rally with the entire student body and faculty was raucous, showing enthusiasm that had never been seen before. The marching band played the school fight song, and players and cheerleaders made short speeches, and Coach Carson thanked everyone for their support. Mr. M.. walked around and through the crowd, both in the bleachers and on the football field, sensing there might be trouble. He knew that the incidents that were occurring were not coincidental. He noticed Mr. Gald among the crowd and made a point to stand next to him. What was he doing at the pep rally, he thought?

When the rally ended and the students and faculty went back to their classrooms, Mr. M.. was waiting for Gald, standing next to his car in the guest parking area. Leaning against Gald's car with his arms folded, Mr. M.. introduced himself to the surprised Gald.

"Can I help you, sir?" Gald asked very sarcastically.

Mr. M.. smiled, "I just wanted to say hello and introduce myself."

"I know who you are; I've seen you around the school," Gald replied.

Mr. M.. looked at Gald and nodded, "So you have. How's your school been? You're here more than there."

Annoyed, Gald motioned for Mr. M. to move, and the sub-teacher opened the car door for him and sneered.

"You don't ask me any questions. You're nothing but a sub," Gald angrily said. "Keep away from me."

As Gald slammed the car door, he tried to start the engine, but it wouldn't turn over. He tried and tried, but still nothing happened. He rolled down the car window.

"Hey, get somebody to help me here; the car won't start," he barked at Mr. M..

Walking away, Mr. M.. didn't turn around and aptly replied, "I'm nothing here; get it yourself."

Watching close by were Leonard Rowdin, Jimmy Jameson, and Zach Breen.

****

Mr. Blankenship was growing very tired of meetings about security and safety as he'd placed all the proper and authorized procedures together with the state police and local sheriff's department, effective on day one of school. Superintendent Canfield set up the meeting with Mr. Gald in his office. Blankenship was not told what the meeting was about but knew that if it had Gald involved, it would not be pleasant.

Canfield, Gald, and Blankenship waited for the subject of the meeting: Mr. M.. The school loudspeaker called out the request for him to report to the principal's office and got some jovial snide remarks from the students about the trouble he was in. Mr. M.. laughed it off and said he'd be right back as a teacher's aide came in to replace him. He walked to the office without any concern. He anticipated this.

Blankenship was sitting behind his desk, and Canfield and Gald were sitting in chairs in front of him. Mr. M.. walked in and exchanged pleasantries, but Gald said nothing. Blankenship cleared his throat.

"This won't take long, Mr. M..," he said. "Mr. Gald here says you did something to his car the other day. He needed a tow to the shop."

Gald interrupted, ". . . and when it got there, the car started right up. They couldn't find a thing wrong with it. You did something."

Superintendent Canfield listened and looked at Mr. M.., who sat motionless. She was growing annoyed at all of this.

"Maybe Mr. Gald here doesn't know how to start his car correctly? Maybe it was a pilot error?" he said, looking at the superintendent as she chuckled under her breath.

"There are cameras all over the grounds. What did the parking lot cameras show?" he asked, looking at Gald.

Gald became irate, and before he could speak, Blankenship answered.

"Nothing. They showed nothing. We saw you walking in the parking lot and leaning against the car. That's all."

Mr. M.. nodded, "Then why are we having this meeting?" he asked, looking at Gald. "I guess we have another exercise in wasting time, right, Mr. Gald?"

Angered, Gald got up to leave and then turned to Canfield, "You better fire that guy," pointing at Mr. M.., then left.

"Have a wonderful rest of the day," Mr. M.. said to Canfield as he stood up to leave. "Mr. Blankenship, I'm always at your service."

Getting in his car and driving home, he noticed he was being followed.

Mr. M..'s house was at the end of a cul-de-sac not far from school. A large old two-story house with an attic looked like a haunted house from the movies. It had a creaky metal gate in the front and a rusted wrought iron fence around the grounds with a driveway and garage on the side. The outside of the house looked as if it was badly in need of a paint job.

As the sun set, a car slowly pulled up in front of the house with three people in it. The engine turned off, and the three, Leonard Rowdin, Jimmy Jameson, and Zach Breen, looked over the house from the car. They were puzzled: this lot where the house used to be a vacant lot that was a play area for them and other kids in the neighborhood. Rowdin even mentioned that he had not noticed a house in that lot weeks ago. Something looked strange.

As the three boys waited and debated what to do, like toilet papering the grounds and house or throwing eggs at the front door, they noticed that no lights were on. Mr. M. was not at home. They got out of the car and noticed that the front gate was open, as was the front door when they got up to it. As Rowdin attempted to grab the door handle, it slowly opened.

The three boys stepped in and were in awe: a huge staircase, wide with fancy handrails, connected the second floor. There was a large room to their right and one to their left. The lights were dim, but there was a noticeable light on the second floor. Jameson, wearing a gray hoodie sweatshirt, took a step towards the staircase when Rowdin shook his head and opened the door to their right, which was the den.

They quietly entered, and one of the candles on the desk suddenly lit, creating a dim hue. They noticed the bookcase-lined walls, fancy mahogany desk and high back chair, and fireplace. Breen looked up and noticed something on the ceiling in the left corner, like a bat or big bird. He pointed to it, and the others looked at it.

The door to the room slammed shut by itself. Bewildered, the boys looked at each other in disbelief. Bogo, Mr. M..'s winged pet, began to fly around the ceiling and was chirping as he flew. The candle in the room started to flicker; then, the room suddenly changed color from a bright orange to a sky blue.

Then, the lights in the room began to turn rapidly flicker, and loud barnyard noises like cows, chickens, and horses deafened the large room. The room then began to sway back and forth. Terrified, the boys grabbed and pulled at one another, panicking as the room suddenly became pitch black. The door became slightly ajar, and the boys ran out but somehow found themselves on the staircase going to the second floor.

Running up the stairs, they ran to their left, down the hallway, and into the first room they came to. Dimly lit, it was ornately decorated with medieval armor, and in the middle of the wall shined a light on a ship's masthead from an old pirate ship. The wooden figure was a woman staring out, and as the boys crept closer, the wooden masthead tilted her head and asked the boys to please take her off of the wall so she could stretch her legs. Laughter was coming from the six suits of armor spread around the room, and suddenly, a hologram of a huge wild black horse appeared, rearing and howling. The boys then ran away from the horse and opened a closet door to find another door in it. They opened that door and found themselves in another room. That room was on the first floor.

As the boys screamed and yelled for help and to get them out, the room got bright, then dark, then a loud crash, and a thick, gooey substance rained on them. A light went on and off again, and another loud crash and mounds of feathers came down, covering the boys from head to toe.

As they turned, running into each other still screaming, they trudged their way through the feathers to the door, and when they opened it, they found themselves on the front porch. They stood there and looked at each other, completely covered in feathers.

****

Principal Blankenship sat in his office thinking about the latest incident. He was discouraged that this had been happening too often and considered resigning. He closed his eyes and prayed, wondering why the school was being punished. The stress of these odd happenings was getting to him. He turned his chair and stared out the window. A knock at his open door startled him. It was Coach Carson.

"Hi, coach, come in," Blankenship said. "How are you feeling?"

The coach, still thinking about the team's exciting win in the state semi-final championship game, nodded and placed his hands in his pockets.

"I think I'm over it now. The boys played hard and never gave up.

Just a fluke field goal," he answered.

The game played in Gainesville went down to the final seconds, and though the opposing team's field goal attempt was tipped, it never went through the uprights for a one-point victory for Atlantic View. The real concern was while they were traveling to the game by bus, a semi-truck came out of nowhere and almost hit the first team bus. It would have caused fatal damage to the three buses. Miraculously, the truck swerved at the last second.

Coach Carson, in a sweat as he watched the truck miss them, was immediately reassured by Mr. M.., who was traveling with them, that everyone was safe and to forget it.

"Mr. M., you say?" Blankenship asked.

Carson nodded, "Yes. He asked if he could ride with us on the first bus. I told him he could." The coach then had a puzzled look on his face. "He also said that the opposing team's quarterback had the flu and was weak but was going to play anyway. We took advantage of that, and it worked. How'd he know that?"

"I don't know. I told Mr. M.. that we were not going to call him for a few days," the principal said.

Carson was surprised, "I think he should be here every day."

"Well . . . why do you say that?"

The coach smiled, "He brings something here to this school. I can't explain it, but it's just something."

Blankenship slowly nodded and pondered what he had just heard.

That afternoon, Mr. M.. stood in Mr. Blankenship's office. The principal called him in for a meeting. The substitute teacher, usually dressed in a dark suit with a colorful t-shirt, was wearing khakis, a peach-colored polo, and flip-flops. His tall stature seemed to take up the whole room.

Blankenship still had the earlier narrow escape on his mind, but he needed to talk.

"A little time off is good, isn't it?" Blankenship asked.

Mr. M.. smiled, "I am not a person that likes time off. I like being useful," he answered. Mr. M. then leaned on the chair in front of him.

"Permit me to be forward if you please," Mr. M.. continued. You are an extraordinary man. The first bi-racial principal in the county, someone who overcame dyslexia and excelled in sports. You should have been on that Olympic team in '02," he mentioned. Blankenship went to Florida State on a track and scholastic scholarship.

"You've accomplished great things; never give up."

The principal was taken aback: no one knew that he overcame dyslexia. How did he know that? He then thought about the latest incident that almost shut down the entire school.

"I don't know what the cause was, but we had another close call this morning. That horrible odor permeated the entire campus. As the students were going to their first-period class, the smell made some of them sick. I was about to get the students to somewhere safe, but it went away. I reviewed the close-circuit films and noticed you were in the quadrangle. I thought I told you we would not be calling you for a few days?"

Mr. M.. looked around the room and focused on Blankenship. He nodded.

"I know. I thought I left my wallet in one of the classrooms."

The principal was annoyed, "Did you?"

"No, it must have fallen out of my pocket in the car," he answered.

"Well, enjoy your time away. We'll call you when we need you," Blankenship replied.

Chapter Seven

A group of students were in the cafeteria waiting for the bell to go to their first period. They were laughing and howling with delight at the three students telling them a most outlandish story.

The three students, Leonard Rowdin, Jimmy Jameson, and Zach Breen, were telling of their experience in Mr. M..'s house. They told of the crazy rooms, the wild lights and noises, the wild horse, the odd bird flying around, and the muck and feathers that covered them. The other students first thought that the three tried drugs, but the three insisted that they never did.

As they described the weird and unbelievable incident, more and more students gathered around to hear. Rowdin lifted his pants leg to show the sticky substance and feather he could not remove. The students laughed harder when he did that. A teacher came over to break it up just as the bell rang.

Ryan, Rozzie, and Rosemary walked away, looked at each other, and laughed. They were going to find Mr. M.. to tell him what went on and get his reaction. Was he subbing today?

Back in the den in his house, Mr. M.. sat at his desk and was reading the writings of Nostradamus, the old seer. Cam, his faithful German Shepard, sat at his feet, and Bogo, his little winged friend, crouched at the right corner of his huge desk. Squeaking, Bogo tried to get Mr. M.'s attention. Without looking up, Mr. M. sighed.

"I was wondering when you were going to show up," he said.

Standing in the middle of the room was an imposing figure. Just over six feet five inches in height, with a slim body, white hair, short-cropped white beard, and moustache, the senior warlock looked around the room and shook his head.

"You're not glad to see me, my boy?" he asked.

Mr. M.. looked up and smiled, "I'm always glad to see you, grandfather."

"Good. I'd be extremely disappointed if you weren't."

Abelgood wore a bright red beret and a black and red robe. Bogo flew onto his shoulder and touched his cheek in an affectionate gesture. He smiled and patted the winged creature on the head, which made him chuckle.

"You know that nonsense you pulled with those boys the other day was not necessary. You could have kept the door closed or just had that black horse make a lot of noise to keep them out. You terrified those boys. Not something I taught you," Abelgood said.

Mr. M. nodded, "I used bad judgment. It was worth it, though."

"Do you have things under control here? What I can see is that this looks like the work or influence of our notorious friend, and I used my friend not in an endearing way," Abelgood said.

Mr. M. sat back, "I cannot figure this one out. The target is a school. That is as heinous and despicable as one can get. Got any ideas?"

"I might. I want you to handle this one by yourself. You've done some great things over the years," the wise old grandfather replied.

"You know, at first, I never approved of your father's marriage to a mortal; he broke the line. But over time, your mother won me over with her sensible, rational thinking and how well she raised you."

Mr. M.. was surprised to hear this. His grandfather never told him how he felt about his mother.

"She put you out there with the mere mortals, you know, schools and even sports. I admired you for the fact that you never used your powers to influence any success you have earned. You failed at things, and that made you better."

Listening intently, Mr. M.. gently stroked Cam as Bogo flew from Abelgood's shoulder and onto the desk. The old sage continued.

"Your mother was a wonderful lady. Smart, practical and she put up with your father. We had many conversations, and they were mostly about you," he said with a smile.

Mr. M.. gently tapped his index finger on the desk as Abelgood spoke. Hearing about his mother was comforting.

"Gambling can be a devastating habit. It was worse with your father; he'd be at the racetrack trying to fix the races, and I'd be right there making sure he didn't. How many Super Bowls did he try to influence? I made sure his powers were weakened. He certainly kept me busy."

Mr. M.. chuckled, "He tried to get me in on Super Bowl Thirty-Four. I wanted nothing to do with it."

"I know that. I was there, too." The grandfather cleared his throat. "I taught you well. Under my tutelage, you've done great things. You saved lives during the Black Plague, helped guide ships across the Atlantic, and done so many smaller things, all for good." Abelgood smiled, "You are still revered in Cornwall. Why don't you go back there?"

Abelgood was referring to the ogre that lived on Saint Michael's Mount near Cornwall, England. The eighteen-foot-tall, shaggy bearded giant terrorized the countryside around the early 500 CE. Gogmagog The Giant would wait until low tide and walk from the island to the village of Cornwall and raid the countryside of cattle and grain. Along with his brother, the equally tall and hideous Cormoran frequently terrorized the diligent, hardworking people.

A farmer's son named Jack, a strong and clever young man, decided to put an end to the giants' pillaging and devised a plan to get them. He knows that one or sometimes both giants come out at low tide, so he decides to get in a boat and surprise them in the cover of night. He runs into trouble when the tide begins to recede as he approaches Saint Michael's Mount, and Gogmagog departs, leaving Cormoran behind.

The terrifying Gogmagog sloshed through the dark water and stood with his huge club, deciding which farm to ravage first. As he approaches Jeremy Brythe's land, a mounted warrior meets him.

The large black stallion was spewing smoke and fire from its nostrils as it reared and loudly whinnied. The rider, dressed in black with a silver helmet and silver metal breastplate, wielding a flaming hot sword and silver shield. Gogmagog was stunned at the sight. His big, round eyes had never seen this before. He began to swing the huge club over his head as the horse kept rearing and snorting fire. The fearless rider pulled his charger around, getting behind the giant and confusing him as the club missed its target. The fire sword pierced Gogmagog's left leg, causing a loud screech in pain as the village residents all came out, sitting on their roofs watching the battle.

The giant's club swung over the rider, repeatedly missing and almost causing the horse to topple over, but the skilled rider steadied the charger and swiftly slammed the fire sword into the ogre's right leg, forcing him to his knees. Cursing and howling, Gogmagog snorted and took a knife from his waistbelt. He was about to lunge when the rider moved away and stretched out, swinging the sword. Looking at the haggard, scraggy, bearded face, the rider swung and severed the giant's head from his body.

Some of the villagers ran to the giant's dead body and began stomping on it as others stood around the mounted hero, showering him with praise and flowers. Farmer Jeremy Brythe offers the hero mulled wine and bread, but someone mentions that young Jack is nowhere to be found. The hero rider immediately takes off for St. Michael's Mount, and the villagers watch in awe as the black stallion glides over the murky waters.

The rider landed on a beach of driftwood that led to some trees that stood before a cave. The armored rider dismounted and went into the cave and saw Jack tied to a spit, and some goats scurried by in fear. The giant Cormoran had his back to Jack, sharpening his knife. Surprised at the sight of the rider. Quietly, the taut ropes were cut away, and Jack was freed. Both mounted the swift charger and returned to the village.

As a celebration was being planned with sweet treats and wine, the loud bellows of Cormoran were heard across the bay, and the villagers were shaking with fear. The hero warrior gave Jack his shield and fire sword and told him that if he got close to using a pickaxe to finish the ogre off. He then mounted the black steed and disappeared.

Abelgood vividly described the incident. It was the first time his grandson used his powers to thwart evil by himself, and the old sage admired the fact that the young hero had left Jack to save the village. There was always a place in Cornwall for him, even today. Grandfather Abelgood figured there was something more going on At Atlantic View High School. The old sage tapped his forehead with his right index finger and nodded.

"You are half-mortal, so there are powers that you have and don't have. You know that," he said.

Sitting up in his chair, Mr. M.. tilted his head slightly to the right, "I know that; I've always known that."

"You have feelings. You also know that you never let feelings get in the way of your birth powers. That has always been the problem with mortals; their feelings decide their fate," Abelgood was referring to his grandson's new friend, Spanish language teacher Isabella Sanchez.

"This young teacher you're fond of, this language teacher, I could understand that, but don't let that get in the way of your judgment. You are more than just fond. Am I right, grandson?"

Mr. M.. smiled, "Yes, you are."

The new teacher stopped him one afternoon and commented on how her classes enjoyed him as a substitute when she needed a day off. She wanted to meet him. The raven-haired, tall, and lean teacher was not only new to the school but also new to teaching. She had just finished her master's in foreign languages and was hired at Atlantic View. Miss Sanchez was concerned about her teaching methods and was doubting herself. Mr. M.. assured her that she was going in the right direction and to keep doing what she was doing. She made an impression with her modest, sincere talk of wanting to make a difference in students' lives. Mr. M.. was smitten. Most of all, he felt as if he had known her before.

"Just remember who you are," Abelgood warned.

Mr. M. nodded, "My father married a mortal."

"Do you know how hard it was for your mother to realize who and what your father was? I spent countless hours with her until she finally understood. She thought she was going insane." The grandfather paused and sighed.

"You are my favorite of all my grandchildren. You take what you have very seriously and understand what I taught you. I never want you to make the wrong decisions."

Bogo flew around the room, landed on Mr. M..'s shoulder, and chirped. Mr. M.. tapped him on the head.

"There's something sinister going on at that school, and I'm going to stop it," he replied.

Abelgood nodded slowly, "I understand. Go to it. If you need me to do this, you will know how to contact me. I say to you, always remember who you are.”

****

The fire department was finishing its inspection. The large stage in the Music and Arts Building was set up for the fall season concert with rustic foliage and new lighting ready for the evening’s performance by the chorus and orchestra.

Smoke was seen coming from the building about three hours before the show began, and there were three custodians behind the stage when the fire started. Not panicking, the workers scurried to pull the alarm and got out.

Principal Blankenship was in his office when the alarm went off. Quickly, he dropped everything and ran out and saw the custodians coming towards him. Smoke billowed out of the rear of the building, and the principal froze, praying no one else was in that building. He was about to run in, forsaking his own safety, when he saw a tall man standing near the building’s rear exit. As Blankenship approached, the tall man sighed and spoke in a low tone.

“I got here just in the nick of time,” the man said without turning around.

The principal was surprised when he recognized the voice.

“I thought you were to be off the campus for a few days,” he said.

Mr. M.. turned around and looked at Blankenship, “I couldn’t find my I.D. badge, so I thought I should come here to look.”

“Now? You came back now?” the principal asked, puzzled.

Mr. M.. smiled, "I'm also going to the concert tonight."

"Oh. Is anyone hurt?" Blankenship asked. "Much damage? Can you tell?"

Shaking his head and looking around, Mr. M. was relieved, "No one hurt and no damage.

"Did you see anyone," the principal, looking around, asked.

Mr. M.. nodded, "Just a few students, but they weren't in the building."

"I have to go in and assess the damage," Blankenship said, looking for the fire marshal.

Mr. M.. shook his head, "No damage. No smoke damage, nothing charred. Nothing."

"I've got to got in with the chief anyway," Blankenship replied.

Blankenship wondered. Mr. M.. always seems to be around when these things are going on or have occurred. The cameras on the grounds might give him a better idea of that.

As cars were parked in the various lots around the Music and Arts Building, Mr. M.. walked around the campus and noticed that the cameras pointing to the building and walking paths were covered with a filmy substance.

After the concert, Mr. M.. went home and watched the recordings of the grounds on his computer, being able to access the video. What he saw was very disturbing. He saw a figure walking towards the Music and Arts Building, then it disappeared. He then saw a familiar figure walking away from the building just before the fire started. He had to get to Blankenship about this.

As the days went by and getting close to the Thanksgiving break, Mr. M.. was called to the high school every day. Mostly, all the students knew him now, and he always conducted classes with some extra obscure facts or things for the students to ponder. He was at the end of the day writing brief reviews of the classes when two students came in to visit.

Rozzie and Rosemary, two students who were in some classes Mr. M.. subbed for, asked if they could come into the classroom, and he gladly obliged. Their friend Ryan was not with them as he usually was, and they told the teacher that there was trouble. Things were not going well with him as he was worried about his grandmother.

Another student stopped by the classroom, Harvey Humble, and made a snide remark about how Mr. M.. was wrong in his lesson about the state of Texas and its fight for freedom from Mexico. Humble was very calm in telling Mr. M.. that he got the entire description wrong.

Rozzie and Rosemary were stunned. Mr. M.. politely told the arrogant student to research what was discussed in class and to get back to him about what he found. Humble mumbled something under his breath and left the room.

The two students thanked Mr. M.. for listening and left the room. As he was leaving the campus, the substitute teacher noticed Principal Blankenship was still in his office. He went in to surprise the principal.

Mr. M.. then suggested that they both look at the recordings and ask Blankenship to see what he saw. Aside from a flock of geese that usually walked through the grounds, Harvey Humble was carrying his instrument case. Surprisingly, Chester Gald appeared to be walking towards the auditorium and then disappeared.

Blankenship was shocked. He thought for a moment and decided he had to consult with his assistant principals. He needed answers.

****

Mr. M.. was at the front door of the modest two-story home on Seaside Drive, about three miles from the high school. A dog was barking as he rang the front doorbell. Answering the door was a woman of about seventy years old using a walker to get to the door. She let the substitute teacher in after asking some questions and invited him into the living room, asking if he wanted tea, but he declined. The dog came over to him, and he patted the pooch on the head. The dog sat next to him.

Ryan Alworth came to the front door of the two-story house he shared with his grandmother after basketball practice. He was incredibly surprised at what he saw and was a bit concerned.

The woman was standing at the stove stirring the stew she was making and checking on the rolls in the oven. He walked over, placed his right hand on her arm, and kissed her cheek. She was standing without any support, and the wheelchair that she needed most of the time was folded and placed in the corner of the living room.

The old woman had a smile on her face, a face that was bright and vibrant. She smiled at her grandson and patted his arm.

"Are you okay, Grandma?" he asked, puzzled at what he saw.

"Okay? Of course, I'm okay," she answered. "I must tell you about a visit I just had. A wonderful visit."

Ryan nodded, "A visit? A doctor? A home nurse?" he asked.

"A nice man came to see me; he just said he goes by Mr. M.. We talked for a long time," she said with a smile. "He knows you from school. Ryan, my grandson, I'm not scared anymore. I'm not afraid to live. See, I'm standing."

Ryan was confused. What did Mr. M.. do, he thought?

"Mr. M.. told me that being anxious about my heart condition only makes things worse. I was angry at the doctors and nurses who practically told me the same thing, but Mr. M.. had a way about him. His calmness was very reassuring to me as he talked, and when he looked at me, I felt a heavy weight disappear from my shoulders. He is an unusual man. A truly kind man."

Ryan nodded and tried to process what she was saying. "What did he say to you."

"He knew about my life, about my losses. He told me I was someone who gave everything and asked for nothing," she said as a tear rolled down her right cheek.

"He knew. He changed my attitude towards things and towards life. I cannot explain what he said to me, but look, I've been walking around the house without any support. I just called some of the ladies who were in the book club I used to go to, and they will be coming over next Wednesday to visit. Maybe starting the club again."

Ryan was astounded. He had never seen his grandmother this way.

Chapter Eight

Principal Blankenship had just finished a meeting with his two assistant principals, who reviewed the video footage prior to the auditorium fire. They agreed that Mr. Gald would need to answer questions as to why he was at the school at that time and even his whereabouts at other times. They had to be careful about this; Gald had friends on the school board.

With weak evidence of any foul play, the principal was ready to call on the superintendent to review the video and then decide if they were to confront Gald. All this had to stop.

The Thanksgiving break was two days away, and the school was anticipating the time off, with mostly all the teachers easing up by not scheduling tests or any extra work. Mr. M.. was subbing for a teacher, a history teacher who was taking two days off before the break. Mr. M.. showed a film about Pearl Harbor and the outbreak of World War Two and started a discussion when a student, Harvey Humble, tried to take over the class.

The arrogant student explained how the Japanese attack was successful and, surprisingly, had amazing insight into the Japanese high command. Mr. M.. was very intrigued by the student's insight and having information not discovered by any historian.

As he was leaving for the day, the sub-teacher was passing a classroom, and his name was called out. It was ninth-grade science teacher Isabella Sanchez. She was about ready to leave for the day when she noticed him walking by. He stopped chatting for a minute.

Earlier in the day, while leading a discussion about Franklin Delano Roosevelt's policies with an honors history class, Mr. M.. had a moment. Two students expressed their dislike of living at home and how strict their parents were. They complained about curfews, and it sounded like they were disrespecting them. Mr. M.. stopped and lamented.

He began to speak softly about gratitude and how it shapes individuals. As he was speaking, a teacher and students stood at the open door of the classroom. In an instant, all the classrooms in the building became silent as Mr. M..'s soothing voice was heard.

He spoke about the tireless efforts that parents make to raise their children, the pain a mother endures in the process of giving birth, and the sacrifices a mother and father make. He recited a line from William Shakespeare's play, *As You Like It*:

Blow, blow, thou winter wind,
Thou are not so unkind
As man's ingratitude;
Thy tooth is not so keen
Because thou art not seen,
Although thy breath be rude.

Freeze, freeze, thou bitter sky,
Thou dost not bite so nigh
As benefits forgot;
Though thou the waters warp,
Thy sting is not so sharp
As friend remembered not.

There was a moment of silence throughout the entire building. The new teacher wanted to thank Mr. M.. for his recital, encouragement, and positive talk when she was feeling a little down. He made a point of telling her that he was glad to hear she was more comfortable with her classes and that things were better. She asked about his holiday plans, and he said he usually relaxes alone. She invited him to her family's Thanksgiving celebration.

Flattered, Mr. M.. thought for a second. He was never invited to anything, ever. He looked at the young teacher, smiled, and told her he would be delighted to attend. He still had this feeling that he knew her from somewhere, somewhere in another time.

As Mr. M.. was about to leave the campus, his name was called out; it was Principal Blankenship. The principal wanted to speak more about the video showing Mr. Gald. Discussing this with the superintendent was delicate, and accusations and assumptions were to be avoided. The two men watched again, and Mr. M.. was puzzled: Mr. Gald was seen, but why wasn't Harvey Humble seen? He was sure the student was there.

****

Sitting in his den and reading, Mr. M.. stopped and looked at Bogo, Cam, and Daisy, his big black swift mare, standing in the room looking at him. He sat back and thought about all their adventures together and their undying friendship. As he thumbed through the pages of an original edition of Herman Melville's masterpiece, Moby Dick, he sat back and stared at the ceiling and thought about the kind biology teacher. Then it hit him: New Orleans in the year 1814.

Mr. M.. stared at the wall to his right and, as if it were a movie screen, watched the events of the Battle of New Orleans in the lavish southern city of the New United States. Bogo leaped onto his right shoulder, and Cam sat up, fixing his gaze on the technicolor wall. Daisy, snorting, watched intently.

He watched the technicolor wall display of a huge scene of hundreds of men armed with muskets and powder horns rallying to General Andrew Jackson's call to defend the city against the invading British.

American dragoons, about a hundred of them, galloped in the direction south of the city to attempt to slow down the imminent advance of eight thousand British regulars. Under extreme pressure, General Jackson barked orders to get people, soldiers, militia, and ordinary civilians to move to set up a skirmish line. Mr. M.., mounted on his stellar black charger, Daisy, volunteered to ride out with a young dragoon captain on orders to slow down the advance.

The young captain, nervous and anxious, was getting his last orders from the flamboyant general and was told that his assignment was vital to the defense of New Orleans. Mr. M.., dressed in a dark green frock coat and pork pie hat, emerged from the briefing with the general and his staff. Waiting for him was Sophia, the eldest daughter of Don Ricardo Sanchez.

Standing by his horse, Sophia held a blue kerchief as she watched him approach. He was to ride with the captain following Jackson's orders to slow down the British advance. He looked at her, smiled, and kissed her right hand before mounting his steady charger. As he sat astride, he bent down so Sophia could tie the kerchief around his right arm like the ladies did for their champions during the Middle Ages.

Daisy, his gallant steed, reared slightly in anticipation, and Mr. M. smoothly doffed his hat to the stunning lady fair. The young dragoon captain rode up next to him, and they rode out into the bramble marsh and heavily wooded land near the Villere Plantation.

Fifty mounted fighters, armed with flintlock pistols and small axes, felled small trees and piled up heavy brushes with thorny bramble blocking any useful path towards New Orleans. A short bridge near the Rodriguez Canal was dismantled, and the parts were thrown into the marsh. To the surprise of Mr. M.. and the captain, a detachment of British regulars were encamped nearby.

Nerves shaking and near panic, the captain became confused, and if it had not been for Mr. M.'s steady demeanor, their mission would have been a failure. The dragoons rode away to warn General Jackson of the advance.

With fire in his eyes, Jackson got word of the enemy's camp and slammed his hand on the table in his tent set up just south of the city. "By the eternal, they shall not sleep on our soil!" Jackson shouted in a rage.

On his stout white charger, Jackson led two thousand volunteers and regulars across the thick terrain to surprise the British camp. Riding alongside the determined general was loyal staff member Pushmataha Mushulatubbee, a Choctaw Indian, and Mr. M.. Within sight of the British camp, Jackson led a three-pronged attack, startling the invaders with precision musket fire and blazing arrows from Choctaw warriors. Armed with two flintlock pistols, Mr. M.. covered the advance of the militia's flanking move and administered it to the wounded. Taking on casualties, Jackson decided to fall back to the Rodriguez Canal out of harm's way.

Mr. M.. tended to the wounded as the short attack resulted in one hundred fifteen wounded and twenty-four killed. The British suffered forty-six killed and over one-hundred sixty wounded.

Jackson's plan has now changed. He saw the invaders regrouping and waiting for their larger force to arrive, so he decided to form a skirmish line with the Mississippi River on his right and the mucky swamp on his left. He called up the rest of his rag-tagged army to position cannons, and to his surprise, he was told they were out of flints and ammunition for the muskets. This fatal dilemma had to be solved quickly.

The wily, fearless General, exhausted but still showing the vim and vigor of a seasoned commander, sipped the hot chicory given to him as the officer's call summoned his staff. The information of low supplies worried the others, but Jackson was reminded by Mr. M.. that the pirate and outlaw, Jean Lafitte, had huge stores of flints, musket balls, and powder. He was immediately ordered to find Lafitte and offer a full pardon for him and his men if they brought the supplies. Mr. M.. galloped post haste back to New Orleans.

Nerves rattled, volunteers stood with slaves and Choctaw braves listening to orders being barked, men being positioned, and the eight batteries of cannons digging in. Rockets seared through the fog, hitting trees above the skirmish line. The British front line was still being brought up, and the thick marsh and swamp stalled their advance, in addition to Mr. M..'s completed task to slow them down.

Reports came back to Jackson that the British were digging a canal from the swamp to the river to move small with troops, but the canal collapsed. Dragging the boats back into the swamp slowed them down, buying time for supplies to reach Jackson's front line. As rocket fire continued, the nervous underdog Americans anticipated a huge fight. Then there was quiet.

General Jackson's steady charger snorted as he slowly rode along the earthworks. Sunrise was near, and the heavy fog blanketed the bayou and swamp, helping the Americans. A few of the men, empty muskets ready, fidgeted as one remarked, 'That's an awfully loud quiet.'

A faint sound was then heard in the distance - bagpipes. The sound sent shivers down the spines of the anxious American defenders, and Jackson, astride his horse majestically exuding command and confidence, assured the men that the purpose of that sound was to do just that.

As the bagpipes got louder, a yell from the marshes and frantic movement rustled the lines as Mr. M.. guided Jean Lafitte and his pirate band along with twenty Choctaw Indians through the mucky swamp to the line of the earthwork with barrels of powder, musket flints, and ammunition. The Americans raised their hats and cheered as the supplies were distributed. General Jackson watched the lines tighten and doffed his hat in gratitude towards Mr. M..

As the advancing British got in range of the Kentucky long guns now fully supplied, Jackson stood tall on a parapet, raised sword in hand. The bagpipes got louder.

"COMMENCE FIRING!" was the command as Jackson waved his sword.

There were thirteen dead and thirty wounded Americans in the aftermath of the victorious battle that lasted about two hours. The wounded, swiftly tended to by Mr. M.. and three female slaves, and one elderly Choctaw man, were recovering at a large infirmary tent set up thirty yards from the earthworks. Mr. M.. was dressing the arm wound of a fifteen-year-old when he was summoned by a sergeant. As he left the tattered tent, he saw Major General Andrew Jackson standing by his horse. The exhausted but stalwart general tipped his hat as Mr. M.. walked over to him.

"To you, sir, I give you my hand in friendship and gratitude. Your determination without any regard for your own safety is more than commendable, and for that, I am eternally grateful," Jackson said to him as the others in the tent looked on.

Mr. M.., sweat pouring down his face, proudly shook Jackson's hand. Without saying anything, he bowed his head slightly in return. As he watched the general go into the tattered tent to see about the wounded, a horse rode up. It was Sophia.

With two large bladders of water attached to her saddle, she dismounted and went over to Mr. M.. He took her hand and kissed it as his sweaty and grimy hand gently caressed hers. She looked at him and smiled.

Mr. M.. stared at the wall as the image disappeared like a movie fading away. He looked at Bogo as his little winged friend squeaked and shrugged his shoulders. He had a sharp, accurate memory, but this beautiful young lady baffled him.

The Thanksgiving celebration was filled with much merriment, laughter, and affection as Maria Elena's family welcomed Mr. M.. warmly. He brought flowers for her mother and two bottles of wine for her father. He visited with her grandparents, who were conversing in fluent Spanish and made a point to visit with all thirty family members. She was pleasantly taken with his gestures and manners.

The festive holiday included such Cuban dishes as Picadillo, a combination of ground beef, potatoes, and olives; Masitas, a crispy pork dish; and Yuca, a root like a potato. Large bowls of Flan, a creamy egg-based custard served with shaved coconut or caramel sauce. There were also three large roasted turkeys and the traditional side dishes.

Mr. M.. spent time with Isabella during the merriment, and her family was captivated by his manners and demeanor. Mr. M.. invited Isabella to go horseback riding the next day, and she gladly accepted.

Just before sunrise, on his swift mare, Daisy, Mr. M.., dressed in a black duster coat, black cowboy hat, black jeans, and fancy cowboy boots, held a brown filly as she approached dressed very stylish wearing a tan flat wide-brimmed hat, black leather coat, jeans, and knee-high riding boots. She easily mounted the filly, and they lazily began to ride in a wooded area with various riding paths. Mr. M.. thought she looked very exotic in her riding outfit.

"Did you ever feel as if you've lived in another time? Another era?" he asked.

Isabella thought it a very odd question and was intrigued.

"It's funny. I have felt out of sorts at times as if I can't explain it in another setting or something," she answered. "Why do you ask?"

Mr. M.. smiled, "I don't know, I think it has to do with, well."

She interrupted him, "Thank you for bringing it up. I could never talk to anyone about it. At times, I feel as if my memory goes back decades or even centuries. It's hard to explain." Isabella felt very comforted by the fact that Mr. M.. wanted to talk about something that had puzzled her for a long time. Most importantly, he understood.

****

Principal Blankenship stood at the entrance of the campus, greeting the students who had returned from the Thanksgiving break. It was going to be an exciting week because the varsity football team was going to the regional playoffs this Friday night, something that has never happened in the school's history. As he nodded and smiled, he noticed Mr. M.. on the other side of the outdoor commons area, casually talking to three teachers. The principal had to speak to the substitute before classes started.

Able to get Mr. M.. away and into his office, Blankenship sat behind his desk and noticed his empty coffee cup full. Odd, 'who filled it?' he thought. Began to tell Mr. M.. that there was a board meeting scheduled that evening, and he was the main topic. The brief discussion ended with the principal relaying that he would be suspended until a decision is made. As Mr. M.. left the office, Blankenship felt bad about having to speak to such a loyal and capable person like that. As he thought and sipped the coffee, he pondered all the weird events happening at the school.

The next morning, Mr. Blankenship thought he was seeing things. He looked out his office window as the students were coming on the campus and noticed something very strange – the students seemed to be all dressed the same. Every student was wearing a black sports jacket, pastel-colored t-shirt, black slacks, and colored sneakers. What was going on?

When the students got to their classrooms, they all removed their jackets, and the pastel-colored t-shirts were tank tops, which were against the school dress code. Simultaneously, every student was told to put their jackets back on or face 'In School Suspension.' No one budged. The astonished principal received word right away of the student mutiny and immediately announced over the intercom system that the dress code would be enforced and that the jackets should be placed back on. Not one student moved.

Principal Blankenship then ordered the entire student body and teachers to the cafeteria for a meeting about all of this.

The students got word that Mr. M.. was going before the board and would be let go. By chance, the threat of a hurricane across the area postponed the meeting even though it was not hurricane season. In protest of this treatment of a popular teacher and a substitute teacher, they banded together to show their support. Phone calls came in, and all the other high schools in the county were experiencing the same oddity.

Students were very vocal about the situation, and Blankenship stood firm on the dress code. Two students speaking for the entire student body declared that they would have no problem staying the entire day in the cafeteria in In School Suspension.

As the superintendent's phone was ringing off the hook, Mr. Gald barged into her office to demand Principal Blankenship's resignation or immediate firing. Superintendent Canfield then issued an order to suspend all classes in every school countywide until tomorrow and for all principals to report to her office as soon as possible.

Mr. M.. sat in his den and began reading The Strange Case of Doctor Jekyll and Mr. Hyde by Robert Louis Stevenson. As he was reading, Cam, his faithful German Sheperd sitting next to him, looked up. Bogo squeaked to get his attention. Mr. M.. looked up and saw Abelgood, his grandfather, standing in the middle of the room. Daisy took a step towards the old man and nudged him forward with his snout.

"Do you always have your horse in the house with you? Odd, wouldn't you say?" Abelgood asked, rubbing the right side of the horse's neck.

Mr. M.. smiled, "I like her around. She is highly intelligent, you know."

The old sage nodded and scratched the side of his head. He sensed his favorite grandson had a dilemma, and though he could not be the remedy, a code of The Warlock, he was always a sounding board. Abelgood picked up a small cannon on the desk that was really a pencil sharpener and looked at it.

"How did you manage to pull that event off? Talk about bringing attention to oneself," Abelgood said. "I'd say that was rather clever."

Mr. M. looked up surprised, "I didn't. It was not anything I caused or even thought of. I'm as surprised as anyone."

Abelgood nodded as if he did not believe his grandson. "So, it just happened?"

"Yes," Mr. M. answered. "It's baffling."

"Well, you caused quite a stir. What now may I ask?" Abelgood asked.

Mr. M.. smiled, "Not sure, but I got a feeling."

Chapter Nine

Principal Blankenship looked over the three students standing in his office. He was a little distracted by his cup of coffee; as he sipped it, it was getting refilled. The boys, Leonard Rowdin, Jimmy Jameson, and Zach Breen, were describing their recent experience at Mr. M..'s house, and the more they spoke, the more bewildered he was.

They described the old house as just appearing out of nowhere, as it stood on a lot that had been vacant for years. The house was dilapidated on the outside but fancy on the inside. They were able to sneak in the back door, and as they walked through the bleak house, a bird-like animal eerily guided them into the den–the quirky, zany den.

Blankenship listened intently as the boys told of being trapped in the room, and then, out of nowhere, a large black horse appeared. The horse whinnied and reared, and then the lights in the room began to flicker. The bird-like creature flew around the room, making a squeaking sound, and suddenly, the horse swooped down low. Before agitated steed.

As the large horse spun around and whinnied, it leaped from the room, going through the large window without breaking it. The three boys held onto each other for dear life. The horse took off into the night sky, swerving and climbing, heading for a cell phone tower, just missing it, then heading for the ocean. At break-neck speed, it plunged into the water and raced under, coming out with a very loud shriek and speeding back towards the house. When they opened their eyes, they were still on the horse and sopping wet back in the den. The lights began flickering again in the room and then went out. In an instant, they were standing on the curb outside the house.

Blankenship was beside himself. This was the most amazing, ridiculous, and hard-to-imagine story ever told. He was sure they were making this up. He sat back and needed a minute to process what these boys had just told him. He asked if they had told their parents about all this, and they said they had not. Good, he thought.

As a few days went on, it was odd that a rescheduled school board meeting had not been set. Some strange things were occurring again at the high school, like classroom doors being locked and the keys not working and an awful stink of sewerage permeating the entire campus and buildings for a few days. The origin was unknown. They hadn't seen Mr. M.. in a few days.

As the students were entering the campus of Atlantic View Elementary School, close to the high school and middle school, crates of Christmas decorations were being rolled out by the custodial staff to display at the school's entrance. Mr. M.. was beginning his second day there, substituting in the fifth grade as he did the day before. As he walked into the school, going to the classroom, he was approached by two students, one a first grader and the other a fourth grader. The substitute smiled at the students as they approached.

"Preston is sad today," the little girl, a first grader, said with panic in her voice.

The fourth grader, her brother, nodded. "He was crying this morning on the bus."

Mr. M.. knew they were talking about their older brother, Preston Stevens, a fifth grader and student he knew.

"The science fair is tonight, and he doesn't have a project," the little girl said.

The substitute teacher saw the panic in both their faces. He thought for a moment and slowly nodded. "Okay, go to class. We'll see about this."

Mr. M.. then sought out the Assistant Principal, explained what he planned to do during lunch period, and was given permission.

Fast food hamburgers, fries, and chocolate shakes were delivered to the school, and Preston and his two younger siblings met him in the gymnasium where the science fair was to be held. Preston looked in awe at all the displays and felt bad and dejected. Mr. M.. took off his jacket, smiled, and confidently said, "Preston, let's get to work!"

Tina and Rodney looked in the large box Mr. M.. brought. Knowing that the prehistoric age and dinosaurs were Preston's favorite subjects, the box was filled with all kinds of items for a diorama. Guiding Preston along, Mr. M.. added a few touches as the boy put together a huge clay volcano and surrounding trees, rocks, and very life-like-looking dinosaurs.

The large diorama on a plywood board was ready for the final part: the combination of dish soap, water, white vinegar, and red/orange food coloring was placed in a large bottle on the inside of the clay mount. With baking soda to be mixed and then poured into the volcano, the eruption would spout.

The three children were in awe at the display, and Preston was alight with utter amazement and could not wait for the science fair to start in the early evening. The three students went to their classrooms while Mr. M..'s work was not done yet.

That evening, Preston, his brother, and sister, along with his mother and grandmother, attended the Science Fair, and as they walked up and down the aisles looking at the exhibits, they kept hearing oohs and ahs two aisles over. A crowd formed around a prehistoric volcano exhibit and watched as the dinosaur figures roared and moved their heads, and the huge volcano erupted, spouting red-orange fire as it made an earthquake-like sound. A grayish substance oozed from the volcano's opening and appeared to emit a light smoke. People applauded, and everyone noticed the name on the exhibit: Preston Stevens.

Standing in the living room of Preston Stevens' house, Mr. M.. looked at the scrawny Christmas tree in the corner of the room. He felt bad about how the tree looked, and with just a point of his right index finger, shiny new ornaments and bright lights replaced the old ones, and a fancy train appeared around the base of the tree. The train locomotive had smoke coming out of its smokestack, and it occasionally whistled. He looked up and pointed again, and a bright star appeared at the top of the tree. He was about to leave but turned around and, with both hands out, slowly brought them down as tinsel adorned the tree's branches. He nodded in approval and left the modest house.

The next few days at the middle school were a bit different for the substitute teacher. He had some early behavior problems that he fixed right away by telling stories about wizards and warlocks, witches, and whirlwinds. Little did the students know that Mr. M.. was reciting his experiences over the many years. The next day and thereafter, Mr. M.. was at Atlantic View High School in his usual position as a substitute teacher.

*   *   *

One afternoon after school, when all the students had left, and clubs and practices were going on, another disturbing incident occurred. As Miss Sanchez was finishing her planning for the next day, she noticed the lights flickering in the room. As she gathered her books and purse, she tried to open the door to leave. Stuck, it would not open. She pulled, still stuck. She went over to the phone in the room to call the office for assistance. The phone was dead. Near panicking, she banged on the door and yelled for help. She yelled louder and began to blackout when the door flew open, and catching her in his arms was Mr. M..

Later, at a diner that was close by, Isabella was relaxed as Mr. M.. ordered two coffees. She declined a slice of strawberry rhubarb pie as the coffee was simply fine. She was confused and baffled about the door being stuck and was mostly embarrassed about it. Mr. M.. assured her that things like that would happen and that she would not have to fret too much about it. As she was again explaining what had happened, he kept thinking this was not an accident; this was done purposefully. The next day, Mr. M.. went into Isabella's classroom before school started and checked the phone. It was working fine. He examined the door; it was locked and unlocked. It worked fine. Did he have to watch her more closely now?

85

The Christmas break was just a week away, and the school was festively decorated. Christmas carols were played in the halls as the students changed classes. Teachers planned class parties for the last day of class, and the holiday break was anticipated. The grading period was ending days before the break, so classes had exams to take. As the exams began, every car siren in the school parking lot went on, blasting the sounds at a deafening pitch. Teachers were confused, and students stopped and complained as the alarms seemed to get louder. Principal Blankenship ran out to the main parking lot and had to cover his ears. Over in the far corner of one of the supplemental lots was a man standing, looking up at the sky. He could not make out who it was and raced in that direction. Suddenly, the alarms stopped.

Standing in the place where the unknown person was, the principal looked all around. That person just disappeared, he thought. There had to be something on the ground's recordings.

The rest of the day was all about the odd alarms. Teachers were very disturbed, and some thought that it was one or two students behind it. Principal Blankenship called for a full faculty meeting the next morning, and attendance was required; no excuses.

Chapter Ten

Mr. M.. had a challenging time in the very beginning. As a boy living in various places, mostly near London, England, and Hartford, Connecticut, he could not understand some things. His father, Basil, was a tall, stately-looking gentleman with a black pencil, thin mustache, and deep brown hair who was always well dressed. There was nothing shoddy about Basil. His mother, Aleta, was tall and slender, with champagne blond hair and blue eyes and a small birthmark on the right side of her neck. A very humble and fort right person, she doted on her only son.

During an invasion force of Roman legions under the Emperor Claudius in 43 A.D., Britannic tribes were trading with the Roman Empire, but internal strife resulted in Caratacus, chief of the Catuvellauni tribe in the southern region, wrestling power away, turning his ire against the conquerors, and resisted their occupation.

Caratacus mounted attacks on the Romans, and fierce battles ensued. He was repelled many times in the two days called the Battle of The Medway and forced to surrender. The Emperor Claudius came and solidified treaties with the defeated tribes, restoring peace. Caratacus escaped. One of the elders of the Atrebates tribe, Verica, assumed leadership. His eighteen-year-old granddaughter, Aleta, was always by his side.

Verica, the gray-haired, wiry-strong leader, had trouble walking, the result of a hip wound from the sword of Caratacus in a battle years before. Aleta assisted the elder as he walked. As the villagers gathered to hear Verica convey the treaty with the Romans, a tall, dark-haired man dressed in chain mail armor stood in front of the group. Aleta took notice.

"Were you in the fight?" she asked the stranger.

The man smiled, "I was there. I want you to take a walk with me."

Aleta looked at her grandfather for approval, and the old man thought for a moment, then nodded. The two walked away from the group of people and slowly walked into the woods nearby.

"You are a warrior. It was close out there," the tall man said.

Aleta looked surprised. "So you were out there?

"I was the one that got you out of the fray to safety," he answered. "I saw spears being thrust all around you."

The young girl stopped walking and said, "You were in the fight? Acton, the man I was to marry, but he was killed by a Roman lance as I tried to save him. I woke up in my grandfather's tent."

"I pulled you from the battle. You were about to be trampled," the stranger said.

The young girl, whose matted, long, dark hair hung down past her shoulders and her torn leather shirt, made her look attractive as they began walking again. The stranger kissed her hand and told her he was going to speak to her grandfather.

Aleta and the young man named Basil were married in front of the entire village two days later. The villagers were puzzled at how this stranger came to them and then the nuptials. It was three weeks later that Abelgood walked into the village and visited Aleta after hearing that his son, Brent, was away most of the time. The old sage, dressed in a forest green tunic under a white shawl, saw that Aleta was with a child. She poured him a cup of mull wine as they sat in front of the fireplace of the two-room house.

"I was very surprised at my son's nuptials," the old man said. "I thought he'd never wed."

Aleta was intrigued, "I have never met anyone quite like him. I only know the people in my village and have hardly ever ventured away from it."

Abelgood began to tell Aleta about his son and how he was is different from other men. How he is descended from what would be called "Enchanters". His son has certain powers that can change things, and the excellence of those powers is for the good. He explained that the family blood line is for honorable deeds that oppose evil. However, his son had strayed at times but, not in a fatal way. Aleta was shocked and confused. What did the old man mean when he said they were called "Enchanters"?

"The child you are about to have will have those powers; I am not sure how effective those powers will be. He must be taught the noble way to use them," Abelgood said.

Aleta absorbed everything Abelgood was telling her. She had heard about spirits and men with strange powers but thought they were forest tales. Now, she was concerned about the child she was going to give birth to in two months.

A boy was born to Basil, and Aleta and Abelgood knew that his son would not be the teacher and mentor the child needed. As the boy grew, learning and being nurtured by his mother, there was a time that Abelgood's wisdom and tutelage had to take over.

*   *   *

The last day before Christmas break was anticipated at Atlantic View High School. Teachers planned easy classes with a food day and holiday movies shown. Principal Blankenship's all-faculty emergency meeting the day before was just his assurance that these strange occurrences that came up were just coincidences and safety was still the focus. He did not want to stifle the festive mood. Some teachers were overly concerned, voiced their concerns, and took the last day off. Mr. M.. was back on campus.

Classes began after the Pledge of Allegiance and short announcements by Principal Blankenship over the school loudspeaker wishing everyone a very safe, Merry Christmas, Happy New Year, and Happy Holidays to all faiths. As the individual classrooms settled and food was being enjoyed, a sudden hideous odor began to permeate the entire campus. It hit every classroom at once, sending some students outside to throw up. Blankenship immediately went over the school loudspeaker and ordered all classes outside. Before the classrooms emptied, the horrid, rancid odor disappeared. There was silence. He then announced that all would return to the rooms.

Mr. M..'s classroom stayed put. Though the odor permeated the entire school, his classroom only got a tiny whiff of it. When the announcement came to leave the rooms, Mr. M.. went over to the window in the classroom and stared out, his left index finger pointing out. He assured the class that it was safe and to continue to enjoy the special day. The feeling in the class was one of comfort, but most of all, they all felt safe.

The next class came in, and the talk was about the terrible odor and how it had just disappeared. Mr. M.. had a few holiday movies available and asked the class by show of hands which one to show as they enjoyed the various foods and treats they brought. The rest of the day went without any problems, and the student body was dismissed for the two-week holiday recess.

Mr. M.. was writing his notes for the teacher about the classes, and he had some students in the classroom just visiting. The phone rang in the room, and it was a request to go to the principal's office. He gathered his things, bid happy holidays to the students, and went to the office.

"I have to ask you a question, and I don't care if you're offended," the principal said as Mr. M.. stood in front of the desk and looked at the coffee cup in the corner.

Mr. M.. smiled, "You can never offend me, and besides, it's not in your nature to offend anyone. So, go ahead."

"Are you behind all this nonsense going on around here? I mean, you seem to be around when things happen. Was that you out by the ball fields when the car alarms went off? I saw someone out there at that time. Was that you?" Blankenship asked.

Leaning on the chair in front of the desk, Mr. M.. nodded, "Yes, that was me."

"And?" the principal asked.

"You asked if it was me, and I answered."

Annoyed, Blankenship pressed on, "Did you do anything that caused that? Are you responsible for these crazy and bizarre happenings?"

Mr. M.. smiled, "Your coffee cup is overflowing."

Blankenship, eyebrows raised, saw the coffee flowing out of the cup and grabbed it, getting the cool liquid all over his desk.

"What the devil . . .," he exclaimed.

He looked up, and Mr. M.. was gone.

That evening, as Mr. M.. was in his den surrounded by Bogo, Daisy, and Cam, the doorbell rang. He walked over to the door and opened it to see Isabella Sanchez standing there with a covered bowl of flan, a creamy custard desert with a caramel topping. Glad to see her, he enthusiastically let her in and escorted her into a parlor room comfortably furnished with two plush couches, two high-backed easy chairs, a fancy oak coffee table, and three pedestal lamps. His guest was thoroughly impressed with the room and

"This room is very exquisite. Wonderfully comfortable. I would guess you spend a lot of time here," she said, smiling and looking the room over.

He looked around the room. Before Isabella came to the door, the room had cobwebs and old furniture, and the faded wallpaper was peeling off. He was pleased with the paintings depicting landscapes that were on the walls. Mr. M.. went into the kitchen and came back with a tray of two spoons and two cups of coffee.

"I wanted to invite you to celebrate Christmas with my family. My whole family celebrates with dinner, much like Thanksgiving. I hope you have no plans. I'd like you to come," she said.

Mr. M.. was flattered. He sipped the coffee, "Your family is very warm and jovial. I usually have no plans for the Christmas season."

"Then you'll come?" she enthusiastically asked.

Mr. M.. thought for a moment as Cam, his German Shepherd dog, came into the room and sat next to Isabella. She looked down and stroked his head and back. He looked at her and smiled.

"Yes, I'd be delighted," he replied.

Isabella had left, and Mr. M.. went back into his den. He chuckled a bit when, before leaving, she commented about hearing a horse whinny. He just said that the house was old, and the wind makes funny sounds at times. He sat at his desk, and Bogo flew onto the right corner of the large, elegant piece of furniture. Bogo shook his head and squeaked. Mr. M.. looked at him and nodded.

"I know. I know. Am I making a mistake?" he asked his faithful friend.

"Yes!" a voice shouted out.

Abelgood was standing in the middle of the room and folded his arms. Mr. M.. knew that when the arms were folded, it was not going to be good.

"Does this horse have to be in the room?" he asked, looking

around. "You have not been listening. This is a good girl. She has a good heart, a good soul, and most of all, she is mortal. I will be extremely disappointed in you if you hurt her," the old sage said.

Mr. M.. shook his head, "I love you, my grandfather. You have taught me much, and I am grateful for it. You forget my own mother was mortal."

"Yes. It took her a long time to understand and even accept what we were. That was a different time, too," Abelgood said.

Bogo leaped onto Mr. M..'s shoulder and affectionately placed his hand on his head.

"I promise you, I will not hurt this lovely lady. I promise," he firmly answered.

New Year's Eve was upon the south Florida community. People and families from the northern states crowded the nearby beaches just before Christmas, and most local families headed to Orlando to enjoy the parks there. Mr. M. had just finished a horseback ride along a driftwood beach close to his house and thought about what he could do for this special time.

Christmas was a wonderful time. The morning started in terrific fashion. The Stevens household awakened to a Christmas morning never imagined. There were three shiny new bicycles near the tree, three brightly wrapped presents for each child, and three presents for their mother and grandmother.

As the children opened their gifts, their grandmother noticed a large red ribbon around the dishwasher in the kitchen. It was a brand new one. Astonished, their mother could not understand any of this. She noticed an envelope under the tree with her name on it. It contained a set of keys and a new keychain. She took the keys, looked out the window, and saw a new Toyota SUV with a big red and green ribbon around it in the driveway.

"How could all this happen? Who was behind this?" mother said in a faint voice.

Chapter Eleven

Miss Isabella Maria Sanchez sat in her classroom, getting ready for the new school day and new year. Was she still having trouble gathering her thoughts of reality or fantasy? Real or dream? She had never had the experience that she thought occurred three days before.

Christmas day had been a wonderful holiday. Mr. M.. came as an anticipated guest, and Isabella's family, enamored by the impressive man, welcomed him as a special guest. He came with gifts for everyone. She thought it strange that he had a gift for each person, young and old; it could not be possible that the duffle bag he came with contained all those gifts. The gifts kept coming out.

Isabella was in awe of her guests' effortless way with her family and friends. After dinner, they all sang Christmas Carols in their native Cuban Spanish, and Mr. M.. sang along. He enjoyed every one, and everyone enjoyed him.

New Year's Eve was always spent with her parents and grandparents. When Isabella's phone rang that morning, the familiar voice told her to be ready for a night out in the town. Excited, she ran out and was able to get an appointment to get her hair done and make-up.

Mr. M.. came to the door of her apartment at 8 o'clock dressed in a black tuxedo, black bowtie, crisp white shirt, and vest. His silver cuff links glistened. He also had a pocket watch and chain. Standing tall and austere, he smiled and was thrilled that she was ready to go. He escorted her to his car, that unusual combination of Cadillac,

Lincoln, and Rolls Royce. He opened the passenger side of the car for her, and she sat in, admiring the wood interior. He started the chic automobile, and it was quickly enveloped in a white-gray mist.

It was early evening, and they were standing next to the car. Isabella was terrified at first, then felt a rush of excitement as she looked around. Mr. M.. and Isabella stood on The Jardin du Champs de Mars with the Eiffel Tower directly in front of them. Crowds were walking along the Avenue Anatole France, and the stunning couple walked with them towards the iconic tower.

The sun was setting, and the revelry permeated the crowd. They walked to the tower, and their reservation for dinner was confirmed and they were escorted to their table in Les Jules Verne, the magnificent restaurant at the top. The city of lights was captivating as the waiters came by with menus, and Mr. M.. ordered champagne and escargot to start. The sunset, and Isabella was totally enchanted by the atmosphere. The waiter came with a sparkling drink and appetizer and recited the menu. Mr. M.. ordered the smoked salmon and scallops plate for two and the hazelnut meringue and coffee for dessert. The wine was an exquisite Alsatian Pinot Blanc, 1910.

The lighted plaza around the tower was filled with revelers and music played by a live orchestra, adding to the occasion. The couple slowly ate their New Year's Eve meal with a light, jovial conversation.

After dinner, they went down to the plaza, walked along the Champs de Mars, and waited for the stroke of midnight. When the clock struck the new year, the orchestra, heard very clearly yet not close, performed Auld Lang Syne; the orchestration played like a magnificent symphony. Mr. M.. took Isabella in his arms and danced to the wonderful rendition. She suddenly noticed that everyone had disappeared, and they were the only ones there. They waltzed as the lights around them glistened. The music stopped, and he looked at her.

The school year resumed after the Christmas break, and it brought three new teachers. The occurrences of the first few months caused three teachers to resign and find work elsewhere. Principal Blankenship was in a bind and had difficulty getting replacements. The day before school was to start, a young lady stood outside his office. Surprised, the principal asked her what her business was, and she went in to discuss the biology position that just become vacant. Miss Carson briefly gave her background, and having no choice, he had to speak to the department chairperson. She was hired.

With two more positions to quickly fill, Blankenship got up to fill his coffee cup and noticed it was already filled as he thought he was sure he had emptied it. He sat back down, and his phone rang. An applicant for the open algebra teacher position was waiting. Mr. Eisenstein walked into the office and spoke of his qualifications. He was sent to speak to the department chairperson. He was hired. Late that same afternoon, Blankenship hired Mrs. Picasano as the new art teacher.

Things seemed to be going smoothly without incident for a few days, but it happened again: the three gates allowing traffic to enter the parking areas were mysteriously locked after almost all the teachers arrived. Traffic at all three gates backed up near the main thoroughfare, and car horns blared in frustration as maintenance crews tried to unlock the gates. Blankenship was out by the main gate as the electronic release did not work, and the secured gate would not budge. The traffic jam became heated when parents began leaving their cars and walking towards the main gate, staring at the principal. The Sheriff's deputies, on foot, quickly raced towards the parents to prevent a hostile confrontation as car horns intensified.

As one parent was about to get in Blankenship's face through the fence, the gate began to slowly open. Everyone standing at the gate stared. At the same time, the other gates began to open. Thye principal very casually looked around, then looked at the angry parents and waved everyone in.

Mr. M.. was subbing for Honors American History and was familiar with the students, all good, astute students. Harvey Humble, a student who has always been a bit smug and a know-it-all, walked into the classroom, gave Mr. M.. a look sideways, and mumbled something. The bright student was not immensely popular but had a following of about five students who were always with him. The substitute teacher watched the snide student stroll to his seat.

The topic for the day was the causes and effects of World War Two. Mr. M.. began by asking the students to open their books to the subject chapter and just listen for a few minutes while he told them about the rise of the Nazi party as the result of World War One. Harvey Humble interrupted. He started a discussion about a country's right to govern itself and the atrocities the world directed at Germany. He defended the Nazi Party and its nationalism. The class was curious as to how Mr. M.. was going to respond. Calmly, the careful teacher opened the discussion to the class, asking for opinions to be backed by facts. Students went at Humble as the topic got heated, with students calling the diminutive student a fascist.

Harvey Humble stated facts about pre-war economics in Germany that were very precise and even surprising to Mr. M.. He carefully articulated the circumstances in post-World War One Germany. The class was in awe of the short speech. The class then looked to Mr. M.. to debate the sharp student, and after a short pause, the substitute teacher began to describe the party's rise and the diabolic way control was taken. Harvey Humble seemed to be stopped, but then, the arrogant student interrupted and angrily went into a factual national socialist Nazi recital. Mr. M.. was astonished.

Finally, to get Harvey Humble to settle down, Mr. M.. gave the class the homework assignment left by the teacher, and the students tried to continue. Just then, the substitute teacher posed a question to the arrogant student, a question he could not answer. The bell rang, ending the class.

As the students were passing through the halls and buildings for their last class of the day, the fire alarms went off, sending many students running to the parking lots. Mr. M.. ran outside and quickly looked around and knew it was a false alarm. He looked over to the music building, where the alarm came from, and the loud blaring noise immediately turned off. Principal Blankenship ran out of the administration building and glanced around. He saw Mr. M.. gathering the students up and getting back to their classes. Later that afternoon, when classes ended for the day, Blankenship sat in his office and stared out of the window. He turned to his desk and noticed his previously empty coffee cup was now full.

The young principal stared at the embossed cup. It was not full a minute ago. He looked up and saw Mr. M.. standing there. Startled, he leaned forward.

"Mr. M.., can I help you?" he asked.

Mr. M.. stood with his right hand in his pocket and nodded, "Don't even think about quitting. Too late now. What happened to the commitment to yourself to see all this through?"

"My comm . . . how do you know that?" the puzzled principal asked.

Mr. M.. smiled, "We talked about it, remember? Stand fast, Mr. B., you'll get through this."

"You know something? I have to say, ever since you arrived, there's been odd, different, unusual things going on. I've often wondered if it's you that's the cause," Blankenship replied.

Mr. M.. nodded, "I guess that's a legitimate statement."

The principal then said something that Mr. M.. anticipated.

"I'm going to take you off our substitute list. Maybe even have you removed altogether. We need a change."

His administrative assistant, Mrs. Sheldon, came to the door and said there was a call for him. It was the superintendent.

The principal looked at Mr. M.. with the meaning of time to leave, and the substitute teacher turned and stepped towards the door and stopped. He was able to catch the gist of the conversation. The phone call was not a pleasant one.

*   *   *

The large room was packed with people. Parents and teachers, and some business owners. Many of the students were out in the parking lot because they were not allowed to attend the emergency meeting. Isabella Maria Sanchez sat in the front row of chairs with her colleagues, waiting for Principal Blankenship to arrive. The school board members mingled with the parents and some teachers.

Superintendent Canfield took her seat in the center of the dais at the front of the large room, and Mr. Gald sat next to her. The room had a low, droning hum of talking when Mr. Blankenship entered with his wife. The room suddenly became quiet.

The principal took a seat at a table to the right of the school board dais by himself as his wife sat in the first row to the right of his table. The gavel slammed the sound block on the tabletop, and everyone was called to stand and recite the Pledge of Allegiance, which everyone did. Then, Mrs. Stallings was asked to read the mantra of the school district while everyone was still standing. The room was asked to be seated while Mrs. Canfield gave her opening address. She cleared her throat and smiled as she looked around the room. She began:

"Our schools face challenges each day. Teachers, students, administrators, and parents, day in and day out, meet those challenges with robust effort and dedication. What has been going on at Atlantic View High School since the beginning of the school year cannot be explained. It has caused some injuries, teachers leaving, and all of us questioning what might happen each day. This must be formally and publicly addressed. Emphasis on our schools in this district stands for fair play . . ..”

As she continued, Mr. M.. slowly and quietly walked through the door, past the sheriff and deputy standing in the back of the room, and made his way to Principal Blankenship’s table. He took a chair against the wall, placed it next to the principal, and sat down. Superintendent Canfield glanced at the table without stopping.

“We stand for fair play and fair treatment each day, never hindering the path to superior education. We take pride in second chances, offering quality education . . ..” She paused, attempted to continue, and noticed the crowd was more focused on the principal and Mr. M.. She turned to the table and the two men.

“Principal Blankenship, is this your representative . . ..”

Mr. M.. interrupted her, “Is this an open hearing?” he asked.

“Yes, it is,” she answered.

Mr. M.. smiled, “I’m a spectator and have taken a seat. A seat here. If there is a problem with this, we’d all like to hear.”

Mrs. Canfield slowly nodded and looked at the principal, “No problem.”

Superintendent Canfield began asking questions:

“Principal Blankenship, we all know that odd, strange things have been going on at Atlantic View High School for quite some time. You have been seriously involved in finding the underlying cause of all of it. Parents, students, our fine sheriff’s department, and we all are concerned. What can happen next?" she asked.

Mr. Gald, sitting with the board, rustled in his chair. He leaned forward.

"I'd like to add . . .." He was cut off by Canfield.

"Let Mr. Blankenship speak, Mr. Gald."

Blankenship clasped his hands and slowly rubbed them, "Thank you, I'd like to answer."

The crowded room got noticeably quiet. The principal gave Mr. M.. a puzzled look and began to speak.

"These events and occurrences are unexplained. Our security cameras on the grounds have not been able to pick up any one person or persons or anything showing cause. The entire campus is concerned each day . . .," he was interrupted.

"So, you have no answers or prevention," Mr. Gald broke in.

Blankenship was surprised at the rudeness. He cleared his throat.

"Prevention? How does one prevent an occurrence when it's unknown? Can one prevent a thunderstorm? A hurricane? No. I can only assure parents and students that safety is our number one priority and that they should take every precaution each day."

Gald spoke up again, "So you have no answers," he repeated.

Superintendent Canfield looked around the room, then at the principal, and was about to speak when a car alarm was heard. It was unusually loud, louder than normal. People started covering their ears. A sheriff's deputy ran in and gave the license plate number of the car, and shocked, Mr. Gald jumped up from his chair on the dais.

"That's mine!" he shouted and ran out of the room.

Canfield waited as the alarm got a bit lower, but it was still on.

"Mr. Blankenship, we, parents, students, the school board, need answers."

The principal, feeling as if the entire board were against him, sat up in his chair, about to answer as best he could, when Mr. M..'s right hand grasped Blankenship's left arm.

"He's finished. He gave you answers. What do you want this man to do? I'll tell you, all of you have no answers either," Mr. M.. interrupted.

The superintendent was surprised at the outburst, and the crowd rustled in their seats. The room got tense.

"Sir, your interjection is not . . .," she was interrupted by Mr. M..

"Is this a hearing? Open to the public?" he asked.

"Yes, but the question was directed at Principal Blankenship, no one else," she answered.

"He doesn't have to answer any more questions, especially when there are no answers," Mr. M.. said and then stood up.

Wearing his usual black suit and a light orange T-shirt, his carriage got the entire room's attention. The crowd could faintly hear the car alarm outside.

"What are you people trying to do to this man, this good man? You're all caught up in these events, and you should be, but blame this man for them? He is doing what any decent person would do, and you all know it. He has restored pride in this school ever since he's been here, and you all know it's been lacking for quite some time. Reading and math scores are up, and the science department is celebrated throughout the state. Teams are winning. When was the last time every team in every sport went to the state? I will tell you, never. Attendance, despite these odd occurrences, has been steady at almost 99 percent each day. He also has kids attending the school. Do you think he is not concerned?" he continued as the crowd and the school board stayed totally silent.

"Instead of sitting on your brains and judging this man on something that has no explanation, you all should be behind him each day. When was the last time any one of you on the school board visited the school except for Mr. Gald, and we all knew his intentions? You get rid of this man, you get rid of success. Most of all, you hurt this man; you hurt the very spirit of this school.

This spirit should be embraced, not tossed out. This is a good man."

Someone started to clap, and then another clapped, and then others clapped, and the entire crowd applauded. Superintendent Canfield turned to the school board, and they all stood up to convene in another room, but they stopped. They have already made their decision. Canfield got everyone quiet, looked at some notes handed to her, and spoke. There was serious talk of students being kept home and even closing the school.

"Based on the situation and these unexplained occurrences, the board has decided to put better effort into Atlantic View High School and put a more precise security plan into action immediately. Principal Blankenship will continue his outstanding duties as principal."

The entire room erupted in applause and cheers; the sheriff and his deputy applauded; all the students outside let out whoops and cheers. Mr. Blankenship looked at Mr. M.. sitting on his left. He reached out to shake his hand, but Mr. M.. smiled, got up, and walked out the side door. Behind him was Miss Sanchez. She hugged him and was about to say something when Mr. M.. smiled.

Chapter Twelve

Principal Blankenship took his regular place at the front of the quadrangle, greeting the students as they came in ready for school. He smiled as he greeted and waved to three teachers walking across the open commons area. He felt relaxed, without pressure, confident.

A winter festival was planned for the upcoming weekend, and the principal, though at ease, could not keep thinking about what might happen. Extra security was provided by the county school board, with a private firm hired to walk the halls and grounds throughout the day and night. Some students felt intimidated by the uniformed guards, but the consensus was their presence was welcomed.

Mr. M.. was scheduled to substitute for Honors English, a challenging class with students who asked a lot of questions, and the discussions were always lively. The first-period class got into a discussion about Charles Dickens as they were reading Oliver Twist. As Mr. M.. was asking students to describe the title character, honors student Harry Humble interrupted and began to engage another student in how Mr. M.. was totally wrong about his assessment of the author and story. The teacher interrupted and calmly said that if there was anything to contribute, to please contribute to the class. Humble ignored the teacher. Mr. M.. paused as the arrogant student began again, proclaiming that the substitute teacher was clueless. Mr. M.. was finally able to shut down the student and insisted that if he had something constructive to say, he could raise his hand.

The class was annoyed at Humble, and the student sensed it. He quieted down, looked around the room, and started to mock the other students, telling them that they were being taught falsities. Finally, Mr. M.. asked the arrogant student to get up in front of the class and continue his rude preaching. Humble refused. The teacher began to pose a question when he was again interrupted. As he was about to scold Humble, the bell rang, ending the period.

That night, while sitting in his den, Mr. M.. thought back to a previous time. He looked at the blank wall to his right and stared as if it was a movie screen. At once, an image appeared as if a movie was starting. A time when he was walking in the Welsh town of Gilfach Goch. The people there were discouraged by the colliery. The owners of the coal mine cut wages, affecting the hard-working families. As Mr. M.. walked the cobblestone streets with the one-story stone house, all built the same, he came upon a boy slowly walking. Mr. was passing the boy, and the youngster tipped his grimy cap and smiled.

"Hallo to you, sir," the boy said.

Mr. M.. looked at the boy who was carrying a tin box with a handle, probably used to carry some food. His face was sooty, and his hands black like the coal he dug. His worn trousers looked like they were patched a few times, especially at the knees.

"You look like a very industrious worker," Mr. M.. said with a smile.

The boy nodded, "Yessir," the boy said proudly.

"You have been working long?"

The boy smiled, "Yessir, since last year. I make four shillings a week now."

Four shillings didn't seem like much, but it was to the boy. They walked together as the boy said he was going home after working sixteen hours in the mines. He was enormously proud of his job.

"Me da-da works in the same mine. He works nights and makes a pound and five shillings a week. I do not see him much," the boy said. "I got a mum and five older sisters too."

Mr. M.. looked at the boy and wondered about his age.

"How old are you, young man?" he asked.

The boy smiled, "Nine years old last March."

"Did you ever go to school? Learn reading and writing?" he asked the boy.

The boy shook his head, "No, but I did learn my letters. My older sister taught me."

Mr. M.. saw how proud the boy was. He spoke with his head up. There was a kind of maturity in this youngster. They walked, and the boy slowed his walk and smiled as he looked at the humble house to their left.

"Well, sir, this is my home. Would you like to come in and have supper with us? I must scrub first, and my mum makes a good mutton roast. We would like to have you," the proud boy said.

Mr. M.. was touched, "Thank you. I appreciate that invitation very much. I must be going, though."

"What's an inva, an invasion?" the boy asked.

Mr. M.. smiled, "Invitation. Well, it just means that a person is polite enough to ask someone, a stranger, to supper or to share a pint. It is a nice gesture."

"You can come in anytime you like. "We have plenty," the boy said with a big grin.

Mr. M.. bowed slightly and put his hand out to shake this young man's hand. The boy smiled and proudly placed his right hand out. The firm grip of the boy was impressive as they shook, and the boy then turned towards the door.

"Hey, what's your name, son?" Mr. M.. asked.

The boy turned and smiled right before opening the door to his home, "Roddy. Roddy Owen."

Years later Mr. M.. returned to Gilfach Goch as the colliery was in the throws of a violent strike. Brisk negotiations and cooler heads prevailed as the owners and workers came to a compromise satisfying both sides and ending the tense days. Upon word of the settlement, the workers, over a hundred of them, marched in the streets singing and praising the young man that represented the workers. When Mr. M.. asked a joyous miner who the young man was, the man proudly exclaimcd, "Roddy Owen."

*　*　*

Atlantic View High School had been quiet for a couple of weeks. Things were calmer with extra security on the grounds and additional security cameras installed. Principal Blankenship was beginning to

111

feel at ease each day as were the students, so much so, that he felt fine with the county relieving fifty percent of the security. Blankenship later found out that it was Mr. Gald that strongly suggested to the board that the detail be scaled back for budget reasons.

There was excitement around the campus as the annual winter festival was planned for the upcoming Friday. Each class, first-year student, Sophomore, Junior, and Senior, creates a themed float to the entire school at the football field and stations are set up around the school providing lunch for everyone.

As the festival neared, Principal Blankenship grew anxious with the feeling that something just might happen. He requested full security for the day. He waited for an answer and got none. The morning of the anticipated festival saw one-hundred percent student attendance and parents were calling during the week for permission to attend. A major league baseball player that graduated from Atlantic View was to be the Grand Marshal and local news was also set to be doing a story on the event.

Mr. M.. was assigned to help with the crowd movement into the bleachers and was out at the football field with Miss Sanchez looking over the area when she said she felt a lot better and more at ease since the school board meeting.

As they walked around the field before classes began, Miss Sanchez was talking about the demeanor of her students and mentioning that it had improved. She was excited for the day and hoped that Mr. M.. would be with her during the festival. There was something comforting about him, she felt. As they walked and watched the food tables getting set up and students carrying signs and props for their floats, Mr. M.. noticed something very odd: Mr. Gald was standing in the west corner of the football field by himself looking as if he was surveying the area. Mr. M.. was about to go over to Gald when he was summoned over the loudspeaker system to go to the principal's office.

Miss Sanchez said she would go to her classroom to greet her students before the first bell and Mr. M.. said he would see her there. The substitute teacher, standing in the principal's office with two other teachers going over the day's protocol, glanced out the window and saw a cluster of students and Gald walking towards the administration building. He was very curious as to why the assistant principal of another school would be at Atlantic View. Principal Blankenship wanted to make sure Mr. M.. knew his position and got annoyed that the substitute teacher kept looking out the window. The principal finally had to ask what the problem was. Mr. M.. blurted out that Mr. Gald was on campus and was concerned. Though he tried to dismiss that, Blankenship continued to talk about security and safety with Mr. M.. nodding though not really listening. The principal paused and Mr. M.. said he had to get to the special education building to assist before going to the football field. Mr. Gald being on campus was disturbing to him.

The football field was finished being prepared with planks and plywood laid to protect the field and vendors were just about all set up. Students went to their first period and the Pledge-of-Allegiance was being recited by the entire school. A brief announcement came over the loudspeaker about the festivities and to remind students to be on their best behavior.

The parking lot was crowded with floats ready to proceed with parents driving them. Mr. M.. was fidgety. He had an unbelievably bad feeling and left the classroom to see Principal Blankenship to have him hold up the start of the festival. He appeared in the principal's office, but he was not there. In an instant, Mr. M.. was standing on the football field as the sheriff's deputies took their positions in the bleachers and around the track surrounding the field.

Glancing around looking for Gald, he noticed some students milled around the goal post on the east end of the field and it di not look good. Of the four boys there, one was Harvey Humble, and he was being jostled around. Three boys were pushing and shoving the arrogant student and even picked him up and turned him upside down. In an instant, Mr. M.. was on the ruckus and the three bullies ran heading to the field house nearby. Humble composed himself, looked at the substitute teacher, and quietly walked away.

An announcement by Principal Blankenship came over the loudspeaker proudly proclaiming the festival was about to begin, and students were to go to the bleachers to their assigned spots. Mr. M.., now standing at his place at the top of the middle of the eastern portion of the stands, noticed the three boys that were bullying Harvey Humble, walking with their class. In that instant as they were walking towards the bleachers, they got their feet stuck on the ground. The three boys started laughing at first, then started to cuss as they could not move. The other students moved around them and some even pushed them. Still, they could not move. A sheriff's deputy came over and tried to get them to move with no luck.

Another teacher came over and as the students were getting backed up as the boys were blocking the path. Finally, they got their feet released but the teacher heard them cussing and pulled them out to be sent to the detention room for the day. The students kept filing past into the bleachers waiting for the festival to begin. The Grand Marshal was standing ready to go to the center of the field accompanied by two sheriff deputies right after Mr. Blankenship was to give opening remarks. The National Anthem was played.

Remarks, waves, cheers, a whistle blew, and the festival was under way. The floats began to roll onto the football field as the first float, a depiction of a baseball field with lights and members of the school's baseball team around the float. The Grand Marshall waving as it goes to the center of the field. As it is making its turn, the other floats depicting science, social studies, math, language arts, physical education, elective courses, followed the large float of the school's administration. Happily waving were Mr. Blankenship and the two assistant principals amid cheers and applause. The occasion and festival enjoyed its fine moments and the air smelled of the delectable aromas of various foods like pizza, tacos, chow mein, hot dogs, hamburgers, corned beef and cabbage, and pastrami and fresh rye bread.

Mr. M.. was glancing about the crow up high atop the bleachers and noticed something. The entire field had all the floats circling and the goal post at the south end of the field was slightly swaying. Mr. M.. hurried down the steps to get to the field as students yelled his name and as he descended, he grabbed a sheriff's deputy and told him to get to the field as soon as he could and to radio to get the floats off the field, now! Then he was gone.

Trying frantically to stop the reaming two floats entering the field amid raucous, enthusiastic cheers and applause by waving his arms, he finally pointed his right index finger at the ground halting the makeshift vehicles. As he quickly glanced around to look for Miss Sanchez, he saw Mr. Gald, extremely animated as he was speaking to the county sheriff. In a flash, he was standing next to the two men and Gald then, to the amazement of the sheriff, froze in his stance.

Mr. M.. could not believe what just happened.

Chapter Thirteen

Emergency vehicles from out of the county and the Florida State Police with the sheriff's people were scrambling to make sure everyone received medical treatment. Crying was still being heard as parents were finally allowed on the campus to be with their children.

Principal Blankenship was speaking with reporters from the local news when a national news truck had just pulled in much to his dismay. The principal, distraught and anxious, did not want to provide any interviews with a national news network. As the news team and cameras came towards Blankenship, they were intercepted. Mr. M.. stepped right in front of the news people, a tall well-dressed young lady carrying a microphone, and a camera operator smoking a cigarette that mysteriously was extinguished. The news team stopped and oddly, could not take a step further as if there was an invisible fence in front of them. They were perplexed at first, became agitated, then irate at being stopped. They then retreated to their news van.

Amid the chaos now calming down, Blankenship, visibly still shaken, walked over to a triage tent set up to look in on four students that were injured. He was grateful that no one was killed. It was a miracle, he thought. He noticed Mr. M.. in the tent speaking with two students, calming them down and reassuring them that they would be fine.

The last of the ambulances left as well as the students and parents as night fell. Standing by himself, Principal Blankenship felt his body tremble as his nerves were about to explode. Startling him was Mr.

M.. standing behind him. The substitute teacher squared his body and gently tapped the principal on the right upper arm with his closed fist in a gesture of support. Saying nothing, Mr. M.. walked away, went to his car, and drove away.

That evening, sitting in his den, Mr. M.. leaned back in the large leather chair and stretched out. He closed his eyes for a moment and when he opened them, he saw his grandfather standing in front of him with Bogo sitting on his shoulder. Cam, his German Shepard, slowly walked over to sit by the desk. Mr. M.. gave his faithful dog a treat and Bogo squeaked so he tossed a treat to the diminutive figure. Abelgood slowly shook his head and stared at his favorite grandson. He felt at odds with himself – he did not help his grandson when he really needed it.

"Thank the heavens that no one was killed," the old sage said as Bogo flew onto the desk. "You did all you could."

Mr. M.. sat back and looked up at the ceiling, then at the old man. He let out a sigh and pursed his lips.

"I did not do enough. I should have seen it coming. I could have stopped it," he answered.

The old man nodded and tried to be realistic.

"You could have. You keep forgetting you are half mortal." Abelgood paused, "You need help. I will get it for you."

Mr. M.. got angry, "No. No help thank you. I will solve this myself. I'm close to getting to the bottom of all this. I'm sure of that."

"You had better hurry, my boy. How long will it be until someone gets fatally hurt?" Abelgood asked.

Mr. M.. looked down at his desk as Bogo quietly jumped onto his right shoulder. He then sat back and let out a low sigh. He had seen things, odd things, over the centuries, but nothing like the happening at school earlier in the day.

As Mr. M.. was closely watching Mr. Gald, he noticed a wavey, eerie field around the football field. It was as if the field, from end zone to end zone, was about to sway back and forth. At once, the entire field, with every float on it, rose about five feet, then swayed from one side to the other and began to sink, shaking as if it was an isolated earthquake. The goal posts tipped over missing Principal Blankenship's float on one end and missing the superintendent's float on the other end. Students and teachers screamed in terror as they were tossed around, many crashing onto the grassy field crushing each other.

Running onto the rocking field, Mr. M.. began grabbing students and with his superior strength, lifted two and three students at a time to safety. The tumult did not affect his balance as he quickly navigated the chaos grabbing anyone he could and getting them off the field. He saw Principal Blankenship struggling to keep his feet to help and in an instant with one arm, scooped him up and slung him over his shoulder at the same time grabbing two others. Getting them to safety, he frantically looked for Miss Sanchez.

Swiftly moving amongst the frantic and harried crowd, Mr. M.. saw the teacher struggling to her feet and attempting to help others as the field still rocked back and forth, up, and down. Screams and howling in terror, students and teachers struggled to get to any stable spot and Miss Sanchez was trying to help, herself losing footing and falling. Mr. M.. appeared next to her as she was about to fall into a large muddy pit and grabbed her arm then lifted her to safety. Exhausted, she collapsed on the grass a few feet away from the tumult, so Mr. M.. dragged her away to a safer area.

In a rage, Mr. M.. leaped onto the rocking field and his body rose a few feet from the ground and with a space opening, slammed his spread-out body down as if to clutch the field. The rocking and wild back and forth movements slowly subsided. As it slowed down, students and some teachers, bruised and battered, stared at the substitute teacher thinking he was dead.

When the mayhem finally calmed and subsided, Mr. M.. got to his feet and immediately got the injured up and away to the side. Sirens were heard, many of them, in the distance. Crying, moaning and low whimpering went through the air as the injured, stunned, and disoriented, tried to regain normal. Mr. M.. knelt by Miss Sanchez, and she saw him and smiled and said she was not hurt but dizzy.

As Mr. M.. vividly recalled the harrowing day, his doorbell rang. Abelgood smiled and nodded.

"I should like very much to meet the fair maiden you have been so taken with," he said.

Mr. M.. shook his head, "Good-bye, grandfather. You know I always welcome you into my home and delight in your presence. Goodbye. Goodbye."

The old sage faded away as Mr. M.. got up to open the door and greet his guest. The door slowly opened, and before Mr. M.. got to it, he saw Miss Sanchez standing there. His face brightened when he saw her. Inviting her in, he led her to the living room, where fresh coffee and two cups were waiting on an end table. She sat down as Mr. M.. poured her a cup and sat opposite her.

"I didn't want to intrude, coming here without calling, but I wanted to thank you for what you did today. With all that was going on, you jumped in and saved a lot of people from serious injuries. Me for one," she said, then taking a sip of the coffee.

Mr. M. slowly nodded, "I could not believe what I was seeing. I've seen many things over the years, but that, well, that was something else."

"I'm still in a bit of a shock as to what happened. How could that happen? I mean, how?" she asked.

Mr. M.. shook his head, "I must find the underlying cause of all this. I keep saying that, and I am not getting anywhere. It's frustrating. Someone will get seriously hurt," he answered, pouring himself coffee.

"It's not for you to get to the bottom of this. What do you mean?" she asked.

Mr. M.. caught himself, "I mean, somebody's got to figure this out."

"I'm scared. I try hard not to think about not going to school now," she said, very troubled. "I keep thinking, what will happen next?"

Mr. M.. nodded, and his dog Cam came into the room and sat

next to her. She patted the dog on his head. Mr. M.. got up and poured more coffee for her.

"Don't ever be scared. Be aware, be looking out. They must stop this," he said.

Surprised at that, Miss Sanchez raised her eyebrows, "They? They?" she asked. "You think it is a 'they'?"

"I don't know. It's possible," he answered. "Why Atlantic View? Why is that high school the target of all this?" he asked rhetorically. I'm going to find out. I'll get to the heart of this."

Miss Sanchez was puzzled at first. She had a strange feeling that Mr. M.. knew more than he was telling. She felt safe with him, yet there was something else. The German Shepherd dog lay down next to her chair as she sat and wondered.

* * *

Atlantic View canceled classes for the rest of the week. State police, along with building engineers and landscape specialists, investigated and examined every inch around the football field, searching for any clues as to what caused the chaos. Mr. M.. appeared near the south goalpost and walked around the end zone. The field looked as if nothing had ever happened. As the substitute teacher walked about the end zone, he noticed something lying in the corner: a small card. He picked it up, and it was an ID card from Chester Gald, Assistant Principal. Was Gald injured in the chaos? Did he try to assist? What happened to him? What was Gald doing there anyway? Mr. M.. had to look at the video of the field, and maybe he would get an idea of all of this.

Sitting at Principal Blankenship's desk, Mr. M.. watched the blurry video of the incident frame by frame. He sat back and stared, and in an instant, the video was clear as day. As the video appeared frame by frame, Mr. M.. acknowledged the principal entering the office without looking up.

"I don't mind you coming into my office, but can you ask first," the principal said, a bit annoyed.

Still staring at the computer screen, Mr. M.. was unfazed, "I might have something here."

Mr. M.. was staring at a frozen frame. As he stared, Principal Blankenship moved to go around the desk to see the screen.

"Oops!" the substitute teacher said as the screen suddenly faded.

School resumed after a three-day suspension of classes. Caution was the order of the morning as the students began to come onto the campus. Slowly walking and not much talking, tension filled the air. Principal Blankenship stood at the school's entrance watching as the students walked in. With his arms folded, he nodded 'hello' to each as they passed by. The Dean of Students, Mr. Carson, was injured in the chaos and still out, was constantly calling the principal to keep of track things.

Mr. M. was called in to substitute for honors history and was told he would have that class for the rest of the week. The students passing to classes were eerily silent. Mr. M.. waited at the classroom door greeting the students as they filed in and was prepared to answer questions. Harvey Humble lazily strolled in and gave the substitute teacher a snide sideways look. He took the wrong seat just before Mr.

M.. walked into the room and waited. As the substitute teacher began to take attendance, he casually requested the arrogant student to get in his correct assigned seat. The student did not move. Mr. M.. then slowly nodded.

"Mr. Humble, why are you so belligerent? What is bothering you?" the teacher asked.

Humble smiled, "I guess I can see a phony like you a mile away. Why would any student pay attention to you?"

"Your opinion. You're entitled to it. Now move to your correct seat," the teacher sternly requested.

Not moving an inch, Humble ignored the request. Mr. M. paused and, with his right hand on his side, slowly moved his right index finger back and forth. Nothing happened. He tried once more – nothing happened.

* * *

Back in his den at his home, Mr. M. sat with his dog, his horse, and Bogo, his faithful companion, around him. Daisy, his horse, stood in front of the huge desk and, reared his head back and stomped his right front hoof. As Mr. M. stared up at the ceiling, he casually acknowledged his visitor.

"Hello, grandfather. I had a feeling you would show up."

The old sage smiled, "You are not supposed to have feelings. Oh, forgive me, you are part mortal."

"You still have that saucy sense of humor, I see," Mr. M.. replied.

Abelgood looked around the large room, "Must you have this equine in the room?"

"Yes," Mr. M.. quickly answered.

The horse whinnied and lifted its head. Mr. M.. chuckled. His grandfather, always his biggest supporter, wanted to take control of the situation but Mr. M. would not have any of it.

"The prom is coming up. There's going to be trouble, you know that. What say you?" Abelgood asked.

Mr. M. nodded, "I think I might be on to something," he replied as Bogo flew onto his shoulder. "I'm close. There must be a way to draw this demon out."

"Then do it. There has been enough damage," Abelgood said as he faded away. "Do it!"

That evening, Mr. M.. went back to the school. He walked around the airy campus and noticed a shadowy figure between two buildings. Appearing at the end of the path, Mr. M.. recognized the figure in the darkness: it was Mr. Blankenship.

Following closely, Mr. M.. watched the principal quietly walk in the darkness. Something did not seem right. Was Blankenship the culprit? No, but there was still some doubt. The huge school cafeteria was the setting for the prom. There was an overwhelming response of students to attend worrying the principal. Darkness covered the entire room as Blankenship made his way to switch on some lights. Startled, he saw Mr. M. standing at the end of the food court, his shadowy figure looked menacing.

"How long have you been here? How did you get in here?" the principal asked angrily.

Mr. M. nodded and said nothing.

"I'm back to beginning to think you're the problem around here. I'll ask you to stop coming to this school. You are banned." Blankenship said.

Mr. M. stood expressionless, "The prom is coming up. You will need me."

Chapter Fourteen

Mr. M. sat in his den in his humble home. He flipped a pen up and down as he sat behind his desk and thought. Disappointed with Principal Blankenship, he thought about all he's done and what trouble lies ahead. He could not begin to think what would happen to those students and teachers.

As he sat, his faithful friend, Bogo, flew up on his shoulder and saw the despair on Mr. M.'s face. Slowly flapping his wings, Bogo placed his left hand on his shoulder and chirped. Daisy, his able charger, whinnied, and Abelgood appeared again. The old sage tapped his forehead with his left index finger and then placed his left palm out over Mr. M.'s head. They were instantly transported to ancient Rome and the Colosseum.

Emperor Domitian, seated next to his wife, Domitia Longina, watched with excitement as five gladiators went up against five barbarian Gauls in a vicious fight with cheers and taunting as the crowd sensed blood. Domitian believes himself to be a divine monarch with absolute power. He personally hand-picked the five gladiators to fight against the barbarians and offered them all fifty pieces of gold to the victors.

Abelgood and Mr. M. stood at the Palatine Hill overlooking the great amphitheater, contemplating whether to enter or not. Fearing for his favorite grandson's life, he wanted to show the viciousness of battle and think about another way to manage the events at the high school. He felt his grandson was overmatched, which could have led to his demise. They then found themselves in the corner of the Colosseum dressed appropriately in tunics and togas, blending in.

Wine and fruit vendors shouted out their goods as the crowd gasped in terror as the barbarians began to overcome the Romans. Loud clanging and slashing sent shivers through the throng. Mr. M. winced as he watched a gladiator go down to one knee to fight off his opponent. Abelgood expressed his sorrow for showing this vicious fight but felt he had to. The crowd let out a loud cheer as the gladiator got up, and Emperor Domitian stood up with a wine goblet in his hand. Instantly, the two found themselves standing in the Roman Forum among the food stands, wine merchants, and garment sellers.

As they walked among the citizens of Rome, Mr. M. could not stop thinking about what might happen. The prom was two days away, and he was going to be needed whether Blankenship knew it or not. They stopped at a shop and got two pomegranate cakes and a lemon drink. They walked around and observed the people. Abelgood knew his grandson was preoccupied in thought as a loud cheer was heard coming from the Colosseum. They were immediately transported to the coast of Naples overlooking the Bay of Naples and the shiny blue-green water glistening. There was a calm feeling when watching the water. Mr. M. said he felt better and wished to go back.

In his den by himself, he opened his eyes, and his grandfather was gone; Bogo was on his shoulder. Watching the gladiator contest showed him something. He never had trouble battling evil. He was a protector. The contests showed that war was turned into a game for the entertainment of the masses and was an atmosphere of sheer violence. What was Abelgood showing him?

Mr. M. sat back and looked towards the front door before the bell rang. It was Isabella Sanchez. She had not seen him for a few days and was worried. He opened the door as Bogo, Daisy, and Camelot disappeared. She smiled and came in, and they sat in the front parlor. He offered her coffee, and she declined.

"I haven't seen you. Are you ill?" she asked concerned.

He smiled, "I'm fine. I just thought of taking a day off. Thanks for your concern."

"I'm on the prom committee, and we're about finished; we're just about ready. I thought you would be involved," she said as his German Sheperd, Camelot, came in to sit beside her. She placed her hand on his head and stroked it.

"I don't think I can. I'm not really a teacher, you know," he answered.

She was surprised to hear that, "You're more of a teacher than I am. You're a big part of that school."

He sighed, "I was told to stay away. So, I'm staying away."

"You'll be my guest at the prom. I can bring a guest, and you're it. I will be picking you up at six o'clock, an hour and a half before it starts. You can't say no," she said, leaning forward. "We have one more day to be ready and to finalize everything. I'm excited about it."

* * *

Principal Blankenship walked around the green campus an hour before students were to arrive for the school day. He was losing sleep over what he thought might happen. By walking around, maybe he could catch any problems before they occur. There will be extra security during the prom, but he was still skeptical.

Three teachers were going to be busy all day finalizing the event, and substitutes were needed. Blankenship had left a note on Mrs. Sheldon's desk not to call Mr. M., but he was indeed needed to help. Stubbornly, the principal would not budge to keep the popular and reliable substitute away.

The day went by smoothly as there were no incidents, just two students getting sick and one rowdy classroom with a substitute teacher. Mr. Blankenship calmed down a little bit as he went about his day. He was puzzled that his coffee cup was full all day, even when he drank most of it. He jotted down some vacation places to take his family when the school year ended. He was in dire need of a relaxing vacation.

That afternoon, three students, Rosemary, Rozzie, and Ryan, went to see Mr. M. at his house. They had not seen him for a few days and were worried. They waited on the front porch. Camelot greeted them, and Mr. M. came out. He was flattered. As the German shepherd basked in the attention of the three students, the substitute teacher assured them that he was all right and they should be excited about the upcoming prom. They helped in setting up being on the student prom committee.

Three more students walked to the house. Leonard Rowdin, Jimmy Jameson, and Zach Breen reluctantly walked up to the porch, hoping nothing would happen. The last time they were there, all mayhem broke loose. They were also concerned. Mr. M. said he would be right back, and he went into the house. Within seconds, he came out with a tray of lemonade and pomegranate cakes. The students commented on how good the dessert was, and Mr. M. said it was from an old recipe. They all hoped he would be a chaperone at the prom, and he said he would think about it. The students left feeling better after visiting one of their favorite teachers.

As far as Miss Sanchez was concerned about Mr. M.., she hoped he would be up to going to the prom. She was excited, so she bought a new dress and shoes to impress him, but she also felt comforted by him being around. Mr. Gald, the assistant principal at the rival high school, showed up looking over the decorations and room setup. He immediately told the teachers that the fire inspector would be around and that all their work was in vain as he would not approve. The giant balloon entrance and carpet were too big, and the plain dark green photo backdrop was not approved by the school board. Mr. Blankenship came in and approached Gald and asked him to leave, but he insisted that he stay until the fire chief showed up.

Concerned, Miss Sanchez was certain that the decorations would be torn down as they were most likely flammable, and the balloons were all right. Mr. Gald was sure everything would be taken down. The fire chief, tall and no-nonsense, looked over the place, was told of the capacity, and signed off approving the entire venue. All the decorations were non-flammable, after all. All was good. Gald was suspicious as the principal walked him out to his car.

It was prom night. The town was abuzz with students getting hair and nails done, last-minute gown adjusting, and tuxedos picked up. The venue was complete; the DJ was getting his equipment loaded.

Principal Blankenship seemed more relaxed and confident that nothing would happen. Extra security was strategically placed, and the principal reviewed the student list many times. As he looked over the chaperone list, he glanced at the parents and teachers and was pleased, but came across Isabella Sanchez as chaperone and her guest, Mr. M.. Oddly, it said just, 'Mr. M.'. Annoyed, he tried to call the teacher, but she was not available.

Cars came up to the school's main gate and were stopped by security to check the trunks and make sure their names were on the list. Once they passed that first point, the cars were directed to a parking area outside the perimeter fence, where each student went through a metal detector and then a hazardous materials scanner. Some parents also complained about all the security issues they were subjected to and complained to one of the assistant principals. Two security guards stood at the entrance to the cafeteria, watching everyone. Three security guards and two sheriff deputies walked around the entire campus.

Miss Sanchez wore a light blue gown off the right shoulder down to her dark blue high-heeled shoes. She has a pearl necklace and pearl earrings with a silver wristwatch on her left arm and a silver bracelet on her right wrist. Her dark hair was long and wavy, and her make-up was done worthy of the red carpet. The last of the chaperones to arrive, she walked in with Mr. M. in her arms, and Blankenship immediately tried to make his way towards them but seemed to be stopped by people talking to him or being called away for his attention to something.

Mr. M. is tall and austere, looking in a white tuxedo jacket, black trousers, a white shirt with a black bow tie, and silver cuff links. Black patent leather shoes completed his attire. His deep, deep brown hair was combed back, highlighting his sky-blue eyes. The couple turned heads as they walked in.

Still annoyed, Principal Blankenship tried to get over to the couple but was constantly stopped for one reason or another. As he was free to approach the guest he didn't want to see, the principal was called to the stage to make a brief opening address to start the party, and a disco light went on, and the music began. As the huge gala went on, Blankenship could not get to Mr. M.. At one point, after Miss Sanchez and Mr. M. came off the dance floor, Blankenship saw his chance, but for some strange reason, his shoes felt as if they were stuck to the floor. He could not move.

Some of the chaperones gathered to talk in a small cluster, and Mr. M. excused himself. He went outside and, lifting his head slightly, was able to see the entire campus in one sight as if it were an overhead photograph. He saw the security guards and sheriff's deputies doing their jobs very efficiently and diligently. All was good.

The party ended before midnight, and the students were all gone; clean up was the next order of business, and it was decided it would be done the next day. As Miss Sanchez and Mr. M. were about to leave, Blankenship tried to approach and was frozen where he stood. Trying to pry his body forward, some of the other teachers looked at him, puzzled. He watched the couple go out the door.

Mr. M. took Mis Sanchez back to her apartment, which was close to school. He took her to the front door, kissed her hand, and turned to walk away. She stopped him, and he came back. She hugged him and told him she was very glad he had gone with her and that she had enjoyed herself very much. He smiled and left.

Arriving early the next morning, Miss Sanchez walked up to the cafeteria to begin cleaning when she saw teachers and a few parents walking towards her. They stopped her and said the entire huge room was fully cleaned, tables put back, floors swept, and decorations packed away. The balloons deflated; every inch of the floor was clean. They told her they had just arrived and went in. Someone must have been there very early or even during the night. Principal Blankenship arrived and was shocked at hearing this. He did not allow anyone access until the morning.

What in the world is going on?

Chapter Fifteen

Abelgood, the old sage and patriarch of the legendary Celtic tribe of Eire, was still gravely concerned about his favorite grandson. He knew that whatever was hovering, aggressively attacking that high school, was a power much mightier than his. He didn't really know how to approach this situation. His grandson is performing admirably under the circumstances. The old sage was perplexed, and the first time in the eons of time he'd been around, he could not put his hand on why this was happening. He trusted his grandson. He trained him and mentored him. This is the first time he's ever feared for him.

Back at his ancient abode on the Isle of Man, Abelgood searched his many volumes of ancient writings. A golden eagle was perched across the room watching, and the old man studied each page. He was able to decipher certain symbols, some diabolical, some biblical. He contacted family members and asked if they had any ideas. One evening, after feeding Ragnall, his Komodo dragon, he suddenly thought about something: the Elspethgrins!

Sorcerers Elspethgrins, a family of warlocks, had been wreaking havoc for centuries. They confuse their foes, and their mischief turns dangerous over a brief period of time. They are on the side of havoc, and their trouble-making has spanned disasters and strife, all in the name of ghastly mischief. In his younger days, Abelgood battled their patriarch, Ofaris, back in the time of the earth's stone age, defeating him numerous times only to have his adversary come back repeatedly, vowing to one day erase Abelgood's family. Ofaris, a long, lanky, pointed-nosed dark wizard, trained his family of warlocks in his image. It's been years since Ofaris has surfaced.

The Elspethgrins were occasionally successful in their mischief, and Abelgood, thinking they were finally defeated, immediately recalled an incident involving his granddaughter, Aestra.

The daughter of his oldest son, Miccah, Aestra was assisting the people of Pompeii during the tumultuous volcanic eruption, helping them flee to safety. Using all her powers to find safe places for the many people, she encountered Kestor, Ofaris' eldest son. The troublemaker blocked streets and shelters, taking Aestra away from her good task. Overpowered, Aestra was about to be pushed away when her cousin, Mynard, appeared and battled the Espethgrin foe.

In the ash and rumbling, Mynard, armed with a fiery steel sword and shield, fought back Kestor's charges at each blow, fighting volley after volley of fireballs and finally taking control of the fierce fight. Aestra hurled fireballs, and being overwhelmed, Kestor disappeared. Aestra and Mynard continued with the evacuation.

Abelgood felt sure that it was someone from the Espethgrin family. The extremely dangerous Kestor. He had to quickly get to his grandson with this deduction.

*　*　*

Principal Blankenship had just come from a meeting with Superintendent Canfield. Ever since those weird events, she insisted on weekly meetings with the principal. Things seemed quiet for a while, and the prom went off very well, but graduation was coming up soon, and it was crucial that that major event was successful. The graduating class was the largest in the school's history, and

Blankenship's job security would be hanging on that.

Back in his office, the principal had a meeting with assistant principals Mullen and Symanski, along with Mrs. Reeder, the social studies teacher in charge of graduation. They went over every aspect and detail of the event, and they were confident it would be successful. The local indoor sports arena was the venue able to accommodate families and guests, and extra security was also going to be present.

The school day was about to begin, and though he was told to stay away, Mr. M. was on the campus. He had met with his grandfather and was certain that Kestor was behind all the tragic mishaps and disasters happening. He needed to be around as he was sure Kestor lurked in the guise of a mortal there. Who? Principal Blankenship saw the substitute teacher and waved him over to his office.

"I was very adamant that you stay away. Since you have been away from this campus, things quieted down. Quieted down a lot. I am not a superstitious man, but I feel more at ease if you weren't here," the principal said, taking the last sip of his coffee.

Mr. M. nodded, "I understand, I really do, but you should know that the things happening around here happened for a reason. There is a definite evil lurking on these grounds, and I'm the only one that can chase it away."

"What? Are we possessed? Do we need an exorcism?" Blankenship sarcastically asked.

Mr. M. leaned forward, "Something like that."

Mrs. Sheldon knocked on the door and went in. She said she was glad to see Mr. M. as a substitute teacher was needed. Blankenship shook his head.

"I'll take those classes today; thank you, Mrs. Sheldon," Mr. M. answered and got up and left.

Annoyed, the principal pursed his lips and looked at Mrs. Sheldon, who was watching Mr. M. walk away. "Do you know a priest, Mrs. Sheldon?"

The classes Mr. M. was substituting for were familiar to him. Social Studies was a fun subject for him, and the students enjoyed the stories he frequently told them. He told those stories as if he was there, they thought. The first period, a senior honors class, was studying World War Two and the section on the Holocaust. After taking attendance and settling the class down, he had an idea.

The class, twenty-one students, patiently waited to begin when Mr. M. told the class to close their eyes and relax. He told them to imagine they were in the year 1943. When they opened their eyes, the class was in the Warsaw ghetto in Poland, watching the uprising of the Jewish citizens against the Nazis. Gunfire and tanks were all around them as the students watched firsthand the fierceness of the resistance fighters. The students stood in the street as Nazi troops marched right through them as if they were not there, as Mr. M. explained what was going on. He said 'we' a few times, slipping, sounding as if he was there. The students bristled with the sounds of fighting and the heavy armor rolling in the streets.

He told the class to close their eyes once again and to imagine them living in 1944. Then, he said to open their eyes, and shockingly surprised, the entire class was standing at the gate of the Auschwitz Concentration Camp.

Standing on the train tracks going into the camp, they observed the sign over the gate in German, translated 'Work Sets You Free.' Frozen in time, the students walked in and observed the horrors of the camp and the atrocities that occurred there. They saw hundreds of emaciated people, victims of tyranny.

One last time, he asked them to close their eyes, and when they opened their eyes, they stood on the cliffs overlooking Utah Beach in Normandy, France. There, Mr. M. described the thousands of allied forces under heavy resistance taking the beaches and scaling the cliffs along the coast. The students could almost hear the chaos as the sea breeze touched their faces. Then, he checked his watch. They closed their eyes and opened, now sitting in their classroom. In silence, the students looked at each other. Did they imagine the trips, or were they there? Did Mr. M. describe those events so vividly as they had their eyes closed, or were they there? The bell rang, and the students filed out, still silent.

* * *

Students were boarding buses to take them to Apex Arena near Miami Beach for graduation practice. Four hundred ten boys and girls, along with ten teachers, were on a twenty-minute trip on seven school buses in a hot, cloudless sky on this May morning. The seniors were very anxious to graduate, as was the talk on all the buses. The lead bus suddenly stopped. The buses behind it stretched to a halt, almost slamming into one another. The lead bus driver got out and looked over the front of the vehicle and saw nothing. The other drivers came out, and the engines of all the buses shut, as well as the doors.

The windows seemed stuck as the air conditioning was off on all the buses. The students and teachers began to panic in the sweltering buses as students were banging on windows and frantically trying to smash the doors out. In the blink of an eye, Mr. M. was driving by and immediately opened the bus doors, and all the windows opened. The students charged out of the boiling buses, and the engines were turned on, air-conditioning blasting out. Mr. M. then got back in his car and led the buses to the arena.

Later that day, Principal Blankenship, the head of school transportation and a mechanic, looked over all the buses. Going over the inside, examining the engines and working the doors and windows, and they found nothing wrong. The principal suggested having those buses taken out of service until a thorough inspection could be made, but the transportation director said they could not afford to have the buses idle. They would have to assume that the buses just had a glitch somewhere, and they would be fine. The principal was apprehensive and had no choice. What was more concerning was Mr. M. on the scene.

Chapter Sixteen

It was graduation day. The entire school was in a jovial mood, especially after the previous days of senior activities like a cookout, a fun day on campus, and the first time a senior taught a freshman class. Mostly, all the teachers were going to attend graduation, and the arena was sure to be crowded with families and friends.

Mr. M. was not at the high school that day. He was spending his day looking over ancient charts and signs, producing any significant clues. He was sure he knew Kestor was behind all this, and the latest incident with the buses was terrifying.

Abelgood appeared and stood in front of him as Camelot barked, and the old man petted the dog on the head. He offered to assist his grandson, but he was turned down. He told the young man that this could very well be the time when Kestor showed himself and his powers were greater. Abelgood proceeded to tell his grandson that the powers of warlocks are unpredictable and, at times, can overpower them. Good must always overcome and defeat evil, and this may be a dire situation. He implored his grandson to ask for help. Mr. M. would not hear it; he was determined to defeat evil at all costs: this was going to stop this last time.

At the end of the school day, the teachers were boarding the buses, which were different from the ones taking the seniors to graduation practice. Jovial talk of vacations and family time spent was heard throughout the buses as the teachers munched on snacks. Principal Blankenship, on the lead bus, was a bit on edge, feeling that trouble was lurking. A few teachers were trying to talk to him, but he seemed distant. His wife sat next to him, holding his hand, giving him a sense of some comfort.

Mr. M. was at the arena well before the students and teachers arrived. He checked out every inch of the vast place and made sure the emergency exits were operational, and if they had to, people could easily get to safety. He looked over the stage with its folding chairs neatly set up in rows and at a slight angle so they could all see the graduates without obstruction. Then, he just waited.

Students arrived earlier than expected, parked in sections designated for families, and mulled around the parking lot, waiting to get into the building. Families were arriving just as the teacher's buses arrived, letting the faculty and administrators out in front of the arena. Blankenship was concerned that the doors were not open and there were no building officials to be seen. As he tugged on the heavy doors, trying three times, the doors opened, and the building manager, smiling and welcoming, let them in.

Miss Sanchez waited outside to round up the students and get them inside out of the sun and humidity. She hoped Mr. M. would be around, but she did not see him worrying her. She was at his house the night before asking him to be at graduation, and he said he would think about it and not let her into his plan.

Students gathered in a room to the left of the long lobby, knowing their places ready to march in. The school orchestra played opening music as the teachers marched in, and the honored guests got seated on the stage, including Superintendent Canfield sitting next to

Principal Blankenship in front. Miss Sanchez and three other teachers got the students in place, ready to march to the ceremonial song, Pomp and Circumstance, and graduation was underway. As the last of the students approached the entrance to the arena floor, Mr. M. stood watching and noticed Mr. Gald walking in. As he was about to stop him from going any further, he noticed another student: Harvey Humble.

Gald looked over at Mr. M. and was about to angrily tell him to leave when rushing right through him specter-like and intercepted Harvey Humble from going in. There stood Mr. Gald, Harvey Humble, and Miss Sanchez. Who was the one?

The rotund student with thick glasses and an arrogant attitude put his hand up and faced Mr. M..

"No one ever saw you in any surveillance videos over the past few months," Mr. M. said, standing erect. "I saw you. It has been you all along," he said to Humble.

Just then, Miss Sanchez walked next to Mr. M., and he tried to keep her away. Gald stood frozen, unable to move. Humble put his right index finger up, pointing to the arena, and Mr. M. quickly appeared in front, intercepting the evil powers and, in an instant, faster than the speed of thought, Mr. M., Harvey Humble, Gald, and Miss Sanchez were transported to Mr. M.'s house in his den away from the ceremony.

Facing each other, Mr. M. watched as Humble turned into Kestor, the evil warlock trying to destroy Atlantic View High School. Tall, lean, ashen face with beady eyes and a pointed chin, his long dark hair flowing down, hitting his shoulders. His eyes turning fiery red, he brandished a fire sword and shield. Terrified, Miss Sanchez cowered behind Mr. M.; Gald stood motionless in the corner.

Bogo appeared and flew at Kestor, and the evil warlock swung his fire shield, knocking it away. Camelot, barking and growling, was ready to pounce, but Mr. M. commanded him to heel. Just then, the walls started to expand, the ceiling slowly rose, and the floor quaked. Mr. M. turned into a massively built warrior with his own fire sword and shield, a golden breastplate as a golden light surrounding him.

The two adversaries squared off. Seeing what he was up against, Kestor began the duel, lunging his sword as Mr. M. parried, and as he was about to overpower, Kestor curled up and turned into a massive fire-breathing dragon snorting and screeching, snapping at the warrior. The demon dragon, about as big as a one-story house, was dark green with a bright orange stripe down the middle of his stomach and orange fins on its back. The searing hot smoke and fire engulfed the room. Daisy, Mr. M.'s faithful charger, appeared, and Mr. M. mounted her as the room got bigger and bigger. The chaos of battle raged as the two slammed into each other. Mr. M. stood back and looked at the beast.

"This is the last time you will ever force your mischief and evil on anyone and anything. You will be sent away for good, for all humanity," he shouted as the dragon lowered its head and made a chuckling sound. "This will be the end."

Miss Sanchez stayed low to the floor and watched as Mr. M. hacked again at the fiery beast, forcing it backward. Daisy whinnied and got up its hind legs, protecting Mr. M. as he got close enough to apply the final blow; the dragon turned into a lizard-like terror on two legs, knocking Daisy to the floor with a mighty thrust of its scaley arms and toppling Mr. M. to the floor. Scrambling up, the lizard-like creature turned back into Kestor. Holding his fiery weapons, he laughed.

"You think you have the power to defeat? You chased me away other times, not this time," Kestor said, snarling.

The two warriors began dueling, slashing, and parrying around the rocking room. Miss Sanchez found a place in the left corner of the room away from the two, terrified and trying to make sense of something no one would ever believe in their wildest dreams. Gald stood expressionless, frozen, not moving. Bogo, Camelot, and Daisy frantically watched.

Just then, as he had his back to the wall, Mr. M. pushed, knocking Kestor's shield away. Dropping his sword, Kestor placed his palms together, extending them away from his body and pointing at Mr. M.. As a bolt of a bright orange laser left the ends of his middle fingers, Mr. M. threw down his weapons and his golden breastplate shot off his chest blocking the laser and crashing into Kestor turning him into a red-orange mist. He was gone.

*   *   *

Standing in the room, he knew so well as a child, Mr. M. stared at his grandfather. He had to dig down with all his might and power to defeat Kestor and needed to see the old sage. Abelgood sat as the large golden eagle flew behind him and perched itself on a stick on the bookcase. He was proud of his grandson.

"I was worried. It was the first time I had been worried in centuries," he said to his grandson. "I was hoping there would be no confrontation, but when dealing with the Elspethgrins, there almost has to be. What is good is we will never see Kestor again."

Mr M, feeling all his powers drained after the titanic fight, was curious, "The fire sword matched his; when he was going in using his total power, my breastplate stopped him and turned him to mist. That was my only defense at that point."

"Your breastplate was gold. Gold signifies divinity, loyalty, and honor. Loyalty and honor are virtues you possess with great zeal. Divinity is something beyond us, yes, even us."

Mr. M. understood and asked if his grandfather had anything to do with his victory. Abel good smiled.

"Just the breastplate," was his answer.

*　*　*

The day after graduation back at school, the last day of the school year, was very lively as most of the students attended, and they congregated around the campus before classes started. The teachers talked about the wonderful ceremony and how well things went. Principal Blankenship was basking in the accolades he was receiving, and he, in turn, lavished praise on the teachers who set the entire graduation up successfully. There was one matter, though: Miss Sanchez was seen at the very end. Where was she, he thought? He called her into his office.

"That was a wonderful graduation. I am more than pleased and incredibly happy nothing went wrong. Nothing bad happened," he said with a smile. I am curious, though; I did not see much of you, and you weren't in your seat?"

The young teacher did not know what to say. She could not tell him what happened; she could not tell anyone. The principal went on to express his appreciation for all her work this past school year. Mr. M. appeared at the principal's doorway and was motioned in. The substitute teacher leaned behind a chair in front of Blankenship's desk and smiled.

"I see you're wearing your usual tie, Mr. M.," Blankenship said sarcastically, as it was always a colored t-shirt and sports jacket as his attire. "You were not there last night; I thought for sure you would be."

Miss Sanchez spoke up, "He was busy, busy saving lives."

Blankenship was puzzled, "What did you do, go into a burning building?"

"Something like that, not quite as exciting," Mr. M. answered.

Picking up his coffee cup that was mysteriously full after he thought he sipped the last drop, he glanced at an email he received early that morning from the superintendent. It said that Mr. M. should be kept on next school year in some capacity. He is highly approved by the school board and received a glowing recommendation from Mr. Gald. He relayed the message to the substitute teacher, and it was taken as a compliment, but he said he could not commit just yet. What was also odd was an email from Mr. Gald offering any assistance if he should be needed. Whatever feud existed was over.

"I'd still like to know some details, especially . . .," he was interrupted by Mr. M..

"After your second cup of coffee, dial this number, 9-Star-Star-9443, extension 000."

Blankenship smiled, "That's a number? Who might that be?" He replied, looking down at his cell phone.

"You will see," Mr. M. replied with a smile.

The principal looked up, and both Miss Sanchez and Mr. M. were gone. He dialed the number, and immediately, a video of the battle between good and evil as Mr. M.'s image came up. Mrs. Sheldon came in, and he waved her over to him to watch the astounding video. The coffee cup was full, and a yellow sticky note was pressed to it. It said: 'Keep doing what you're doing. Great things to come.'

At the end of the final school day, students said goodbye, and hugs went around for everyone; Mr. M. appeared in Miss Sanchez's classroom. She sat at her desk and was glad to see the substitute teacher standing by the doorway. She smiled as he came in, but her mind and body were still reeling from the night before.

"Can you tell me all about, well, who are you really?" she asked, more curious than ever.

Mr. M. smiled, "I'm a friend. There are some things I cannot explain or reveal, but let's say I'm a friend."

"Did all of that really happen, or was it a wild dream? I still can't understand any of it," she said.

Mr. M. nodded, "It happened. You see, there are things since the beginning of time that happen for reasons, some reasons we can't explain. I know this, though: there is good and evil in the world, natural or supernatural. I'm here to try and stop the evil from occurring. I don't know why Atlantic View High School was chosen, but it won't be bothered any longer. The chaos and mayhem stopped last night."

Mis Sanchez was still curious, "We don't know your name; you go by Mr. M.. You must have a name."

He avoided the question and looked around the classroom. He smiled as he looked at posters of Madrid, Barcelona, Cadiz, and Lisbon on the walls.

"Spain and Portugal. I think that would be a nice trip soon; I haven't been in Spain since 1938," he said.

"Will I ever see you again?" she asked.

Mr. M. smiled, "Possibly, I'm in many places at times. I'm very flexible."